19

JUNIOR

CLASSICS

Published by
Rupa Publications India Pvt. Ltd 2016
7/16, Ansari Road, Daryaganj
New Delhi 110002

Sales centres:
Bengaluru Chennai
Hyderabad Jaipur Kathmandu
Kolkata Mumbai Prayagraj

This is a work of fiction. Names, characters, places and incidents are either the product of the author's imagination or are used fictitiously and any resemblance to any actual person, living or dead, events or locales is entirely coincidental.

P-ISBN: 978-81-291-3953-5
E-ISBN: 978-81-291-4325-9

Third impression 2023

10 9 8 7 6 5 4 3

Printed in India

Contents

The Adventure of the Cardboard Box

Arthur Conan Doyle

It was a hot day in August. Baker Street was like an oven and the glare of the sunlight on the yellow brickwork across the road was painful to the eye. My friend Sherlock Holmes lay curled upon the sofa, reading and rereading a letter which he had received that morning.

'Watson,' said my friend suddenly, 'have you read in the newspaper about a remarkable packet sent through the post to Miss Cushing, of Cross Street, Croydon?'

'No,' I replied. 'I saw nothing.'

'It is under the financial column. Would you read it aloud, please?'

I picked up the paper and read the indicated paragraph.

Miss Susan Cushing, living at Cross Street, Croydon, has been a victim of a revolting practical joke unless a more sinister meaning can be attached to the incident. At two o'clock yesterday afternoon a small packet, wrapped in brown paper, was handed in by the postman. Inside was a cardboard box filled with coarse salt. On emptying this, Miss Cushing was horrified to find two human ears, apparently quite freshly severed. The box had been sent from Belfast the previous morning. There is no indication as to the sender, and the matter is even more mysterious since Miss Cushing, who is a maiden lady around fifty, has led a most retired life, and has so few acquaintances that it is a rare event for her to receive anything through the post. Some years ago, however, when she resided at Penge, she let apartments in her house to three young medical students, whom she was obliged to get rid of on account of their noisy and irregular habits. The police are of opinion that this outrage may have been perpetrated upon Miss Cushing by these youths, who owed her a grudge and who hoped to frighten her by sending her these relics of the dissecting rooms. This theory seems probable since one of these students is, to the best of Miss Cushing's knowledge, from Belfast. The matter is being actively investigated and Mr Lestrade, one of our smartest detective officers, is in charge of the case.

'Now for our friend Lestrade,' said Holmes as I finished reading. 'I had a note from him this morning, in which he says:

I think that this case is very much in your line. We have, of course, telegraphed the Belfast post office, but a large number of parcels were handed in on that day and they have no means of identifying this particular one. The box is a half-pound box of honeydew tobacco and does not help us in any way. The medical student theory still appears to me to be the most possible, but if you have a few hours to spare I will be happy to see you here. I shall be either at the house or in the police station all day.

'Well, Watson? Can you run down to Croydon with me for a case?'

'I was longing for something to do.'

'You shall have it then. Ring for our boots and tell them to order a cab. I'll be back in a moment when I have changed my dressing gown.'

A shower of rain made the heat far less oppressive in Croydon than in town. Holmes had sent a telegram so that Lestrade, as lean, strong

and well-groomed as ever, was waiting for us at the station. A five-minute walk brought us to Cross Street, where Miss Cushing resided.

It was a very long street of two-storey brick houses, neat and prim, with stone steps and little groups of aproned women gossiping at the doors. Halfway down, Lestrade stopped and tapped at a door, which was opened by a small servant girl. We were ushered into the front room where Miss Cushing was seated. She was a calm-faced woman, with large gentle eyes and greyish hair curving down over her temples on each side.

'I won't have those dreadful things in here, Mr Lestrade,' Miss Cushing said, as we entered. 'I wish that you would take them away.'

'I have no doubt that you have been annoyed more than enough already over this business, madam,' said Holmes, in his soothing way.

'Indeed I have, sir. I am a quiet woman and live a retired life. I am not used to seeing my name in the papers and to find the police in my house. If you wish to see them you must go to the outhouse.'

The outhouse was a small shed in the narrow garden which ran behind the house. Lestrade went in and brought out a yellow cardboard box, with a piece of brown paper and some string.

Holmes looked at the articles one by one.

'The string is highly interesting,' he remarked, holding it up to the light and sniffing at it. 'It is a piece of tarred twine. Miss Cushing has cut the cord with scissors, as can be seen by the double fray on each side. This is of importance.'

'I cannot see the importance,' said Lestrade.

'The importance lies in the fact that the knot is left intact and that this knot is of a peculiar character.'

'It is very neatly tied. I had already made a note of that,' said Lestrade complacently.

'So much for the string, then,' said Holmes, smiling, 'Now for the wrapper. Brown paper, with a distinct smell of coffee. Address printed

in rather straggling characters: "Miss S Cushing, Cross Street, Croydon". Written with a broad-pointed pen and with very cheap ink. The word "Croydon" has originally been spelled with an "i", which has been changed to "y". The parcel was directed, then, by a man—the printing is distinctly masculine—of limited education and unaware with the town of Croydon. So far, so good! The box is a yellow, half-pound honeydew box, with nothing distinctive save two thumb marks at the bottom-left corner. It is filled with rough salt of the quality used for preserving hides for commercial purposes. And fixed in it are these enclosures.'

He took the two ears out as he spoke and examined them minutely. Finally he returned them to the box once more and sat for a while in deep meditation.

'You have observed, of course,' he said at last, 'that the ears are not a pair.'

'Yes, I have noticed that,' Lestrade said. 'But if this is a practical joke of some students from the dissecting rooms, it would be easy for them to send two odd ears as a pair.'

'Precisely. But this is not a practical joke. Bodies in the dissecting rooms are injected with preservative fluid. These ears bear no signs of this. They are fresh, too. They have been cut off with a blunt instrument, which would hardly happen if a student had done it. Again, a medical mind is likely to choose rectified spirits, certainly not rough salt. We are investigating a serious crime.'

A vague thrill ran through me as I listened to my companion's words. Lestrade, however, shook his head like a man who is only half convinced.

'There are objections to the joke theory, no doubt,' he said, 'but there are much stronger reasons against the other. We know that this woman has led a most quiet and respectable life at Penge and here for the last twenty years. Why on earth, then, should any criminal send her the proof of his crime, especially as, unless she is a very skilled actress, she does not understand it?'

'That is the problem which we have to solve,' Holmes answered, 'I shall set about it by presuming that my reasoning is correct and that a double murder has been committed. One of these ears is a woman's, small, finely formed and pierced for an earring. The other is a man's, sunburned, discoloured and also pierced. These two people are presumably dead or we would have heard their story by now. Today is Friday. The packet was posted on Thursday morning. The tragedy, then, occurred either on Wednesday or earlier. If the two people were murdered, who but their murderer would have sent this sign of his work to Miss Cushing? Why did he send Miss Cushing this packet? It must have been to tell her that the deed was done or to give her pain, perhaps. But in that case she would know who it is. If she knew, why should she call the police in? She should have buried the ears if she had wished to shield the criminal or reveal his name if she does not wish to shield him.'

Holmes sprang to his feet and walked towards the house.

'I have a few questions to ask Miss Cushing,' he said.

'In that case I'll leave you here,' said Lestrade, 'for I have another small business to attend to. You will find me at the police station.'

A moment later Holmes and I were back in the front room, where the expressionless lady sat sewing. As we entered she looked at us with her frank searching blue eyes.

'I am convinced, sir,' she said, 'that the parcel was not meant for me at all.'

'I am almost of the same opinion, Miss Cushing,' said Holmes, taking a seat beside her. 'I think that it is more than probable—'

He paused, and I saw him staring with eagarness at the lady's profile. Both surprise and satisfaction could be read for an instant on his eager face.

'You have two sisters, I believe.'

'How did you know that?' cried Miss Cushing.

'When I entered the room, I observed that you have a portrait of three ladies on the mantelpiece. One of the ladies is you, while the others are so like you that there could be no doubt of the relationship.'

'Yes, you are quite right. Those are my sisters, Sarah and Mary.'

'And here at my elbow is another portrait, of your younger sister, in the company of a man who appears to be a steward by his uniform. I observe that she was unmarried at the time.'

'Yes, she was married to Mr Browner a few days later. He was on the South American shipping line when that was taken but he was so fond of her that he couldn't bear to leave her for so long. So he got into the Liverpool and London boats.'

'Ah, the Conqueror, perhaps?'

'No, the May Day. Jim came here to see me once. That was before he broke his promise; later he would always drink when he was ashore and even a little drink would put him out of his senses. Ah! That was a bad day when he took a glass in his hand again. First he argued with me, then he quarrelled with Sarah and now that Mary has stopped writing we don't know how things are going with them.'

It was evident that Miss Cushing felt very deeply about the subject. She gave us many details about her brother-in-law, the steward. Then she wandered off on the subject of her former lodgers, the medical students, and gave us a long account of their crimes, with their names and those of their hospitals.

'About your second sister, Sarah,' Holmes said. 'I wonder, since you are both maiden ladies, why you do not stay together.'

'Ah! You don't know Sarah's temper or you would not wonder so. I tried it when I came to Croydon but we parted two months ago. I don't want to say a word against my sister, but she was always interfering and hard to please.'

'You say that she quarrelled with your Liverpool relations.'

'Yes, and they were the best of friends at one time. She went there to live in order to be near them. And now she speaks rather harshly about Jim Browner. The last six months that she was here she would speak of nothing but his drinking and his ways. I suspect that he had caught her interfering and given her a bit of his mind and that was the start of it.'

'Thank you, Miss Cushing,' said Holmes, taking down Sarah's address and rising.

'Goodbye, and I am very sorry that you should have been troubled over a case with which, as you say, you have nothing to do.'

There was a carriage passing by as we came out and Holmes hailed it.

'How far to Wallington?' he asked.

'Only about a mile, sir.'

'Very good. Jump in, Watson. We must visit Sarah Cushing while the iron is hot. Just pull up at a telegraph office as you pass, cabby.'

Holmes sent off a telegram and for the rest of the drive lay back in the carriage. Our drive pulled up at a house, which was not unlike the one that we had just left. The door opened and a grave young gentleman in black appeared on the step.

'Is Miss Cushing at home?' asked Holmes.

'Miss Sarah Cushing is extremely ill,' he said. 'She has been suffering since yesterday from brain symptoms of great seriousness. As her medical adviser, I cannot allow anyone to see her. I suggest you to call again in ten days.'

He slipped on his gloves, closed the door and marched off down the street.

'Well, if we can't, we can't,' said Holmes, cheerfully. 'I only wanted to look at her. However,

I think that I have got all that I want. We should go to a decent hotel now. We will have some lunch and afterwards we shall visit Lestrade at the police station.'

By the time we reached the police station the afternoon's hot glare had softened into a mellow glow. Lestrade was waiting for us at the door.

'A telegram for you, Mr Holmes,' he said.

'Ha! It is the answer!' He tore it open, read it and crumpled it into his pocket. 'That's all right,' he said.

'Have you found out anything?'

'I have found out everything!'

'What!' Lestrade stared at him in amazement. 'You are joking.'

'I was never more serious in my life. A shocking crime has been committed.'

'And the criminal?'

Holmes wrote untidily

a few words upon the back of one of his visiting cards and handed it over to Lestrade.

'That is the name,' he said. 'You cannot arrest until tomorrow night at the earliest. Come on, Watson.'

We strode off together to the station, leaving Lestrade still staring with a delighted face at the card which Holmes had thrown him.

'The case,' said Sherlock Holmes as we chatted that night in our rooms at Baker Street, 'is one where we have been forced to reason backward from effects to causes. I have asked Lestrade to supply us with a few details which he will only receive after he has secured his man. That he may be safely trusted to do, for although he is absolutely devoid of reason, he is as tenacious as a bulldog when he understands what he has to do, and indeed, it is just this tenacity which has brought him to the top at Scotland Yard.'

'Your case is not complete, then?' I asked.

'It is fairly complete in essentials. We know who the author of the revolting business is, although one of the victims is unknown.'

'I presume that this Jim Browner, the steward of a Liverpool boat, is the man whom you suspect?'

'Oh! It is more than a suspicion. Let me run over the principal steps. We advanced towards the case with an absolutely blank mind. We were simply there to observe and to draw inferences from our observations. What did we see first? A very calm and respectable lady, who seemed quite innocent and a portrait which showed me that she had two younger sisters. It instantly flashed across my mind that the box might have been meant for one of these. I set the idea aside as one which could be disproved or confirmed at our leisure. Then we viewed the contents of the box.

'The string was of the quality which is used by sailmakers on ships. When I observed that the knot was one which is popular with sailors, that the parcel had been posted at a port and that the male ear was pierced which is much more common among sailors than landsmen, I was certain that all the actors in the tragedy were to be found among our seafaring classes.

'I observed that the packet was addressed to Miss S. Cushing. Now, although the older sister's initial was "S" it might belong to one of the others as well. I therefore entered the house with the intention of clearing up this point when I suddenly stopped. The fact was that I had just seen something that surprised me and at the same time narrowed the field of our inquiry immensely.

'As a doctor, you are aware, Watson, that there is no part of the body which varies as much as the human ear does. Each ear is as a rule quite typical and differs from all others. I had looked at the ears in the box with the eyes of an expert and had noted their bodily structure unusual features. Imagine my surprise, then, when on looking at Miss Cushing I realize that her ear match exactly with the female ear which I had just looked at. There was the same shortening of the pinna, the same broad curve of the upper lobe, the same convolution of the inner cartilage. Essentially, it was the same ear.

'Her sister's name was Sarah, and their address had until recently been the same. It was quite obvious how the mistake had occurred and for whom the packet was meant. Then we heard of this steward, married to the third sister, and learned that he had at one time been so intimate with Miss Sarah that she had gone up to Liverpool to be near the Browners, but a quarrel had afterwards divided them. This quarrel had put a stop to all communications for some months, so that if Browner had addressed a packet to

Miss Sarah he would undoubtedly have done so to her old address.

'And now the matter had begun to clear up. We had learned of the existence of this steward, an emotional man, of strong passions—you remember that he threw up what must have been a very senior position in order to be nearer to his wife—subject, too, to occasional fits of hard drinking. We had reason to believe that his wife had been murdered and that a man—very likely a seafaring man—had been murdered at the same time. Jealousy, of course, at once suggests itself as the motive for the crime. And why should these proofs of the deed be sent to Miss Sarah Cushing? Probably because during her residence in Liverpool she had some hand in the events which led to the tragedy. You will observe that this line of boats visits Belfast, Dublin and Waterford; so that, presuming that Browner had committed the deed and had embarked at once on his steamer, the May Day, Belfast would be the first place at which he could post his terrible packet.

'A second solution was at this stage obviously possible, and although I find it exceedingly unlikely, I will state it. An unsuccessful lover might have killed Mr and Mrs Browner and the male ear might have belonged to the husband. There were many serious objections to this theory but it was imaginable. I therefore sent off a telegram to my friend Algar, of the Liverpool force, and asked him to find out whether Mrs Browner was at home and whether Browner had departed in the May Day. Then we went on to Wallington to visit Miss Sarah.

'I was curious to see how far the family ear had been reproduced in her. Then, of course, she might give us important information, but I was not optimistic that she would. She must have heard of the business the day before, since all Croydon was ringing with it, and she alone could have understood for whom the packet was meant. However, it was clearly our duty to see her, so we went. We found that the news of the arrival of the packet—since her illness dated from that time—had such an effect on her as to bring on brain fever. It was clearer than ever that she understood its full significance.

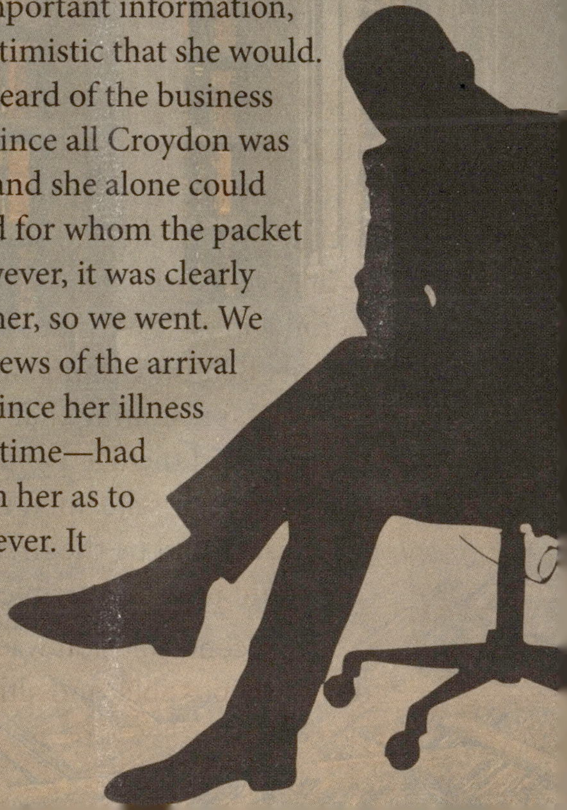

'Our answers were waiting for us at the police station, where I had directed Algar to send them. Nothing could be more conclusive. Mrs Browner's house had been closed for more than three days and the neighbours thought that she had gone to see her relatives. Browner had left on board the May Day and I calculate that she is due in the Thames tomorrow night. When he arrives he will be met by Lestrade.'

Sherlock Holmes was not disappointed in his expectations. Two days later Holmes received an envelope from the Scotland Yard detective.

'Lestrade has got him all right,' said Holmes, glancing up at me. 'This is what he says:

My dear Mr Holmes:

In agreement with our scheme I went down to the Albert Dock yesterday at 6. p.m., and boarded the S.S. May Day. On inquiry, I found that there was a steward named James Browner on board. I found him seated on a chest with his head in his hands. He is a big powerful chap who, at first, jumped up when he heard about my business. But then held out his hands quietly for the handcuffs. We will not need any more evidence, because he has made a statement of which I've enclosed a copy. I am obliged to you for assisting me in my investigation. With kind regards,

Yours very truly,

G Lestrade.

'This is his statement as made before Inspector Montgomery at the Shadwell Police Station.

"Have I anything to say? Yes, I have a great deal to say. I've not been able to sleep since I did it. Sometimes it's his face, but mostly it's hers. The white lamb, she must have been surprised when she read death on a face that had always looked with love on her before.

"But it was Sarah's fault, and may the curse of a broken man set the blood rotting in her veins! I know that I went back to drink. But she would have forgiven me if that woman had never entered our door. Sarah Cushing loved me until all her love turned to poisonous hate when she realized that I thought more of my wife's footprint in the mud than I did of her whole body and soul.

"There were three sisters. The oldest was a good woman, the second was a devil and the third was an angel. Sarah was thirty-three and Mary was twenty-nine when I married. We were happy when we set up house together and in all Liverpool there was no better woman than my Mary. Then we invited Sarah to stay for a week and the week grew into a month.

"Sometimes if the ship was held back for cargo I would spend an entire week at home and in this way I saw a great deal of my sister-in-law, Sarah.

It seemed to me sometimes that she liked to be alone with me or tried to persuade me out for a walk, but I never paid attention to that.

"One evening when I returned from the ship I found that my wife was out, but Sarah was at home. 'Where's Mary?' I asked.

'She has gone to pay some accounts. It's an insult to me that you can't be contented with my company for so short a time.'

'That's all right, my girl,' I said, extending my hand towards her in a kindly way but she took it in both hers in an instant and they burned as if they were in a fever. I looked into her eyes and I read it all there. I frowned and drew my hand away. Then with a mocking laugh, she ran out of the room.

"From then on Sarah hated me. I never said a word to Mary because I knew it would grieve her. After a while I began to notice a change in Mary. She had always been so trusting and innocent, but now she became queer and suspicious, wanting to know where I had been, what I had been doing, whom my letters were from, what I had in my pockets and a thousand such things. We had ceaseless fights about nothing. Sarah and Mary were inseparable. I can see now how she was plotting and manipulating and poisoning my wife's mind against me but I could not understand it at the time. Then I began to drink again. She had a reason to be angry with me now and the gap between us grew wider. Then this Alec Fairbairn came in and things became worse.

"He first came to see Sarah. He was a smart chap, who had seen half the world and could talk of what he had seen. For a month he was in and out of my house and it never crossed my mind that any harm might come of his tricky ways. But something made me suspect and from that day I lost my peace.

"I had suddenly entered the parlour and as I walked in at the door I saw a light of welcome on my wife's face. But when she saw who it was it faded again, and she turned away with a look of disappointment. There was no one but Alec Fairbairn whose step she could have mistaken for mine. If I had seen him then I would have killed him, for I have always been like a madman when I lose my temper. Mary saw the devil's light in my eyes and she ran forward with her hands on my sleeve.

'Don't, Jim, don't!' she said. 'Sarah,' I said as I went into the kitchen,' 'Fairbairn is never to enter my door again.' 'Oh!' she said, 'If my friends are not good enough for this house, then I am not good enough for it either.'

'You can do what you like,' I said, 'but if Fairbairn shows his face here again I'll send you one of his ears for a keepsake.'

"That evening she left my house. She took up a house just two streets off and let lodgings to sailors. Fairbairn used to stay there and Mary would go round to have tea with her sister and him. I followed her one day and as I entered the door Fairbairn got away over the back garden wall. I swore to my wife that I would kill her if I found her in his company again and I led her back with me, sobbing and trembling. There was no trace of love between us any longer. I could see that she hated me and feared me.

"Well, Sarah found that she could not make a living in Liverpool, so she went back to live with her sister in Croydon and things went on much the same as ever at home. And then came this week and all the misery and ruin.

"We had gone on the May Day for a seven-day voyage but were held up for twelve hours. So I headed home. I hoped that my wife would be glad to see me so soon. As I turned into my street, a cab passed me and I saw her sitting beside Fairbairn, chatting and laughing.

"From that moment I was not my own master. I ran after the cab with a heavy oak stick in my hand. Without being seen, I followed them to the railway station and set off for New Brighton behind them. At New Brighton I saw them hire a boat and I rowed behind them.

"There was a bit of a haze and you could not see more than a few hundred yards. We were a long way from the shore when I caught up with them. The haze was like a curtain all round us and the three of us were in the middle of it. I shall never forget their faces when they saw me. She screamed out. He poked at me with an oar because he must have seen death in my eyes. With my stick, I crushed his head like an egg. I would have spared her, perhaps, but she threw her arms round him, crying out to him and calling him 'Alec'… I struck again and she lay stretched beside him. I pulled out my knife and—well, there! I've said enough. It gave me a kind of savage joy when I thought how Sarah would feel when she had such signs as these of what her interfering had brought about. I tied the bodies into the boat and sunk the boat. I knew that the owner would think that they had lost their bearings in the haze and had drifted off out to sea. I joined my ship without a soul having a suspicion of what had passed. That night I made up the packet for Sarah Cushing and next day I sent it from Belfast.

"You can hang me or do what you like with me but you cannot punish me since I have been punished already. I cannot shut my eyes because I see those two faces staring at me. For pity's sake, don't put me into a cell alone, sir."

'What is the meaning of this, Watson?' said Holmes seriously as he laid down the paper. 'What object is served by this circle of misery and violence and fear? It must tend to some end, or else our universe is ruled by chance, which is unthinkable. But what end? There is the great standing perennial problem to which human reason is as far from an answer as ever.'

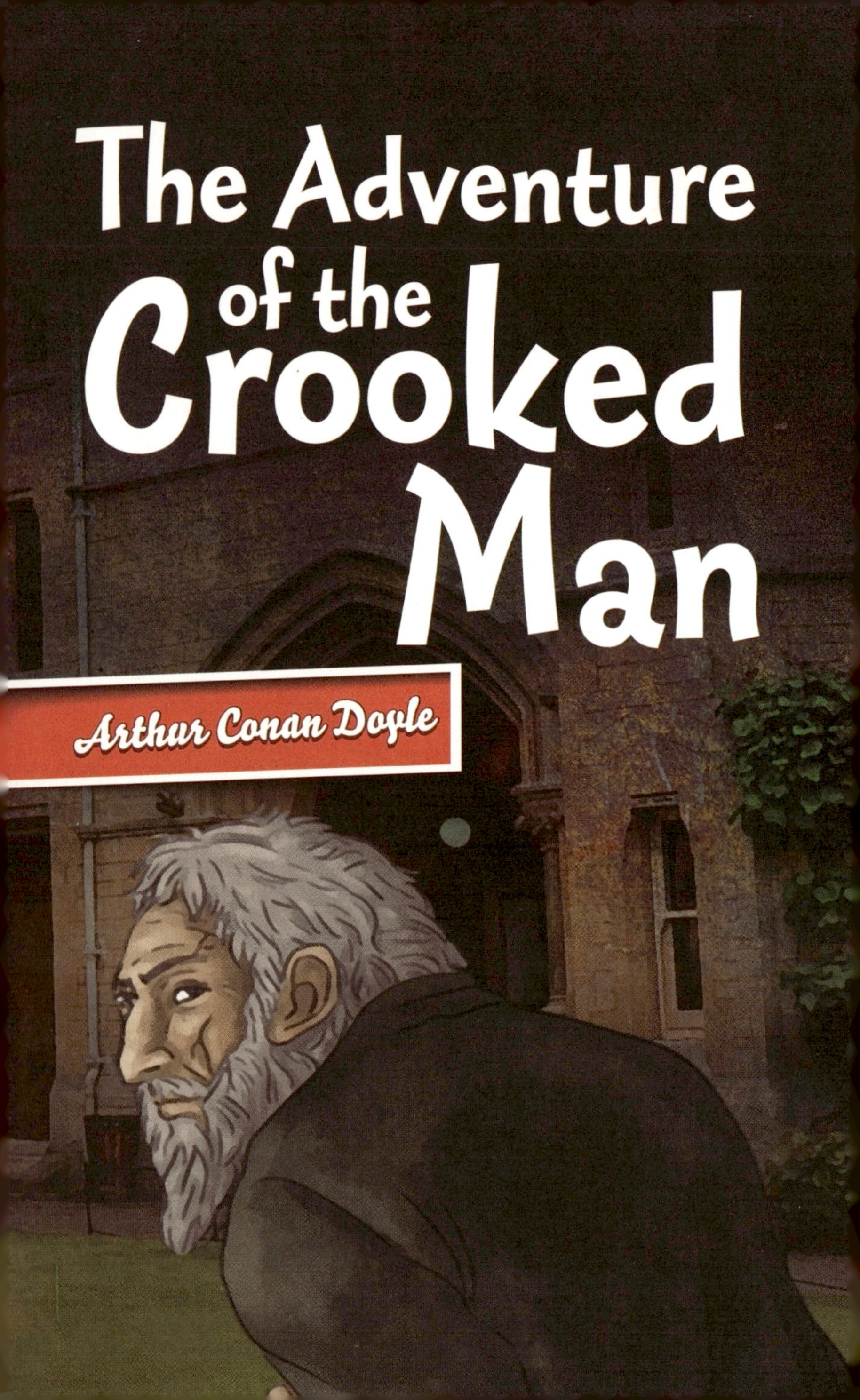
The Adventure
of the
Crooked
Man
Arthur Conan Doyle

One summer night, a few months after my wedding, I was seated by my fireplace smoking a pipe and reading a novel. My day's work had been a tiring one. My wife had already gone upstairs and the servants had also retired. I had risen from my seat when, suddenly, I heard the bell ring.

I looked at the clock. It was a quarter to twelve. I went out into the hall and opened the door. To my great surprise Sherlock Holmes stood on my doorstep.

'Ah, Watson,' he said. 'You look surprised, and no wonder! Could you put me up tonight?'

'My dear fellow, please come in,' I said. 'I shall be delighted if you will stay.'

Holmes sat down and smoked for some time in silence. I knew that nothing but important business would have brought him to me at such an hour, so I waited patiently for him to talk.

'I see that you are professionally rather busy just now,' he said, glancing keenly at me.

'Yes, I've had a busy day,' I answered. 'It may seem very foolish in your eyes,' I added, 'but I don't know how you arrived at it.'

Holmes laughed quietly to himself.

'I have the advantage of knowing your habits, my dear Watson,' he said. 'When your round is a short one, you walk and when it is a long one, you use a carriage. Your boots, although used, are by no means dirty. I am, therefore, sure that you are at present busy enough to justify the use of a carriage.'

'Excellent!' I cried.

'Elementary,' he said. 'It is one of those instances where the reasoner can produce an effect which seems remarkable to his neighbour because the latter has missed the one little point which is the basis of the conclusion. At present, I hold in my hand several threads of one of the strangest cases which ever confused a man's brain and yet I lack the one or two which are needed to complete my theory. But I'll have them, Watson, I'll have them!'

For a brief moment his eyes sparked and a slight glow sprang into his thin cheeks.

'I have already looked into the matter and have come close to the solution,' he said. 'If you could come with me in that last step you might be of great service to me.'

'I will be delighted.'

'Very good. We will then head to Aldershot tomorrow.'

'Now, if you are not too sleepy, I will give you a sketch of what has happened.'

'I was sleepy before you came but am completely awake now.'

'You may have read an account of the matter. It is the supposed murder of Colonel Barclay, of the Royal Munsters, at Aldershot, which I am investigating.'

'I have heard nothing of it.'

'It has not excited much attention yet, except locally. The facts are only two days old. Briefly they are these:

'The Royal Munsters is, as you know, one of the most famous Irish regiments in the British army. It did wonders both in Crimea and the Mutiny and has since that time distinguished itself upon every possible occasion. It was commanded up to Monday night by James Barclay, a brave veteran, who started as a full private, was raised to commissioned rank for his bravery at the time of the Mutiny and lived to command the regiment in which he had once carried a musket.

'Colonel Barclay had married at the time when he was a sergeant and his wife, whose maiden name was Miss Nancy Devoy, is the daughter of a former coloured sergeant in the same corps. Mrs Barclay has always, I understand, been as popular with the ladies of the regiment as her husband was with his fellow officers. I may add that she was a woman of great beauty, and that even now, when she has been married for more than thirty years, she is still of a beautiful appearance.

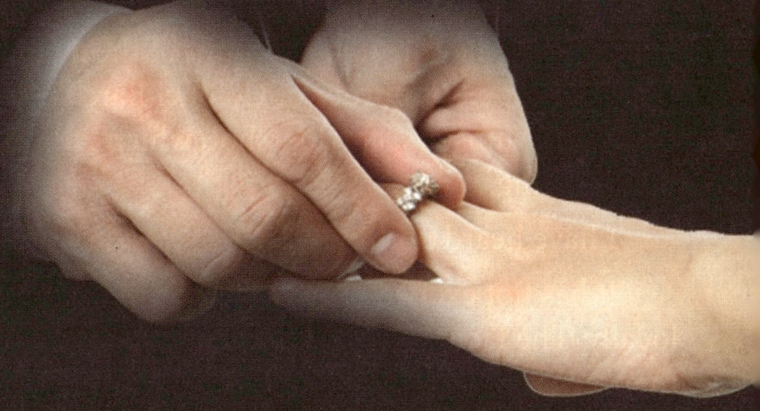

'Colonel Barclay's family life appears to have been a uniformly happy one. Major Murphy, to whom I owe most of my facts, assures me that he has never heard of any difference between the pair. On the whole, he thinks that Barclay's devotion to his wife was greater than his wife's to Barclay. He was acutely uneasy if he were absent from her for a day. She, on the other hand, though devoted and faithful, was less obviously affectionate. But they were regarded in the regiment as the very model of a middle-aged couple. There was absolutely nothing in their mutual relations to prepare people for the tragedy which was to follow.

'Colonel Barclay seems to have had some strange traits in his character. He was handsome, friendly old soldier in his usual mood, but there were occasions on which he seemed to show himself capable of considerable violence and vindictiveness. However, he never seems to have behaved so towards his wife. Another fact, which had struck Major Murphy and three of the five other officers with whom I spoke, was the depression which he sometimes suffered from. When the mood struck him,

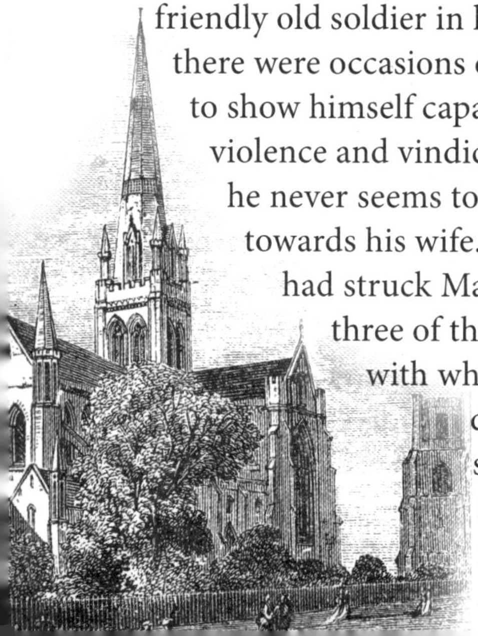

he would sink into deep gloom for many days. He also disliked being left alone, especially after dark.

'The first battalion of the Royal Munsters has been stationed at Aldershot for some years. The colonel occupied a villa called Lachine, about half a mile from the north camp. The west side of the house is not more than thirty yards from the highway. Apart from the couple, a coachman and two maids were the sole occupants of Lachine. The Barclays had no children, nor was it usual for them to have resident visitors.

'And now for the events that took place at Lachine between nine and ten last Monday evening.

'Mrs Barclay was, it appears, a member of the Roman Catholic Church and took an interest in the establishment of the Guild of St George, which was formed for the purpose of supplying the poor with cast-off clothing. A meeting of the Guild had been held that evening at eight and Mrs Barclay had hurried over her dinner in order to be present at it. The coachman heard her assure her husband that she would be back before very long. She then called for Miss Morrison, a young lady who lives in the next villa and the two went off together to their meeting. It lasted forty minutes and at a quarter-past nine Mrs Barclay returned home, having left Miss Morrison at her door as she passed.

'There is a morning room at Lachine which faces the road and opens by a large glass folding-door on to the lawn. The lawn is thirty yards across and is only divided from the highway by a low wall with an iron rail above it. On her return, Mrs Barclay went into this room. The blinds were not down, for the room was often used in the evening. Mrs Barclay lit the lamp and then rang the bell, asking Jane Stewart, the housemaid, to bring her a cup of tea, which was quite unlike to her usual habits. The colonel had been sitting in the dining room but hearing that his wife had returned he joined her in the morning room. The coachman saw him cross the hall and enter it. He was never seen alive again.

'The tea which had been ordered was brought up after ten minutes but the maid, as she approached the door, was surprised to hear her master and mistress having a furious argument. She knocked but did not receive any answer. When she turned the handle she realized that the door was locked on the inside. Naturally, she ran down to tell the cook and the two women with the coachman came up into the hall and listened to the dispute which was still raging. They all agreed that only two voices were to be heard, those of Barclay and of his wife. Barclay's remarks were soft and unexpected, so that none of them were clear to the listeners. The lady's, on the other hand, were most bitter and when she raised her voice could be plainly heard. "You coward!" she repeated over and over again. "What can be done now? Give me back my life. I will never so much as breathe the same air with you again! You coward!" The conversation ended in a sudden terrible cry in the man's voice, with a crash and a piercing scream from the woman. Convinced that some tragedy had occurred, the coachman rushed to the door and strove to force it, while scream after scream issued from within. Unable to make his way in, he ran through the hall door and around to the lawn. One side of the French window was open, which I understand was quite usual in the summer time, and he passed without difficulty into the room. His mistress had stopped to scream and was stretched insensible upon a couch, while with his feet tilted over the side of an armchair and his head on the ground near the corner of the fender, was lying the unfortunate soldier stone dead in a pool of his own blood.

'Naturally, the coachman's first thought, on finding that he could do nothing for his master, was to open the door. But he could not find the key anywhere in the room. He went out again,

therefore, through the window and returned with a doctor and a policeman. The unconscious lady, against whom naturally the strongest doubt rested, was taken to her room. A careful study of the scene of the tragedy was made.

'The unlucky veteran had suffered from a pointed cut some two inches long behind his head, which had evidently been caused by a violent blow from a blunt weapon. It was not difficult to guess what that weapon may have been. On the floor, close to the body, a wooden club with a bone handle was found. The colonel had a varied collection of weapons from different countries and the police believed that the club was from among his trophies. The servants denied having seen it before, but among the numerous curiosities in the house it was possible that it may have been overlooked. Nothing else of importance was discovered in the room by the police, except for the inexplicable fact that the missing key was not found either on Mrs Barclay's person or on that of the victim or in any part of the room. Eventually, the door had to be opened by a locksmith.

'That was the state of things, Watson, when on Tuesday morning I, at the request of Major Murphy, went down to Aldershot to assist the police.

'Before examining the room I cross-questioned the servants and learnt some of the facts which I have already stated. There was one thing in the case which had made the deepest impact both on the servants and the police. This was the distortion of the Colonel's face. It had set, according to their account, into the most terrible expression of fear and horror. It was quite certain that he had seen his fate and that it had caused him the utmost horror. The lady herself, who was suffering from an acute attack of brain fever, could provide no information.

'From the police I learned that Miss Morrison denied having any knowledge of what had caused the ill humour in which her companion had returned.

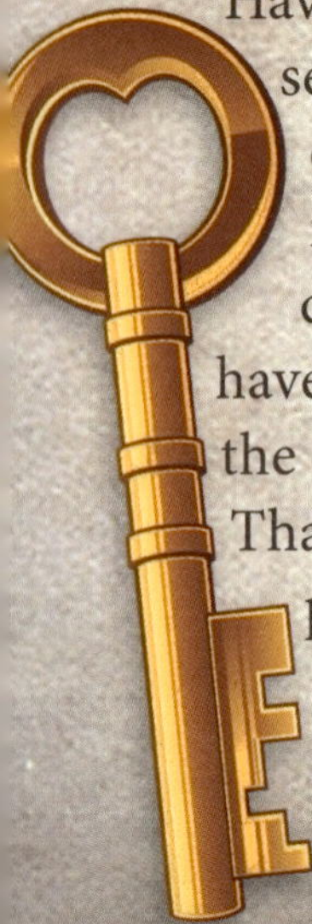

'Having gathered these facts, I tried to separate those which were crucial from others which were merely incidental. The most important point in the case was the disappearance of the door key. It must have been taken from the room. But neither the colonel nor his wife could have taken it. That was perfectly clear. Therefore a third person must have entered the room. And that third person could only have come in through the window. You know my methods of inquiry, Watson.

I discovered that there had been a man in the room and he had crossed the lawn coming from the road. I was able to obtain five very clear results of his footprints: one on the road itself, at the point where he had climbed the low wall, two on the lawn and two very faint ones upon the stained boards near the window where he had entered. He had apparently rushed across the lawn, for his toe marks were much deeper than his heels. But it was not the man who surprised me. It was his companion.'

'His companion!'

Holmes pulled a large sheet of tissue paper out of his pocket and carefully unfolded it upon his knee. The paper was covered with the tracings of the footprints of a small animal. It had five well-marked paw pads, an indication of long nails and the whole print might be nearly as large as a dessert spoon.

'It's a dog,' I said.

'Did you ever hear of a dog running up a curtain? I found clear traces that this creature had done so.'

'What can it be, then?'

'Not any creature that we are familiar with. I have tried to reconstruct it from the measurements. Here are four prints where the beast has been standing still. It is no less than fifteen inches from its fore foot to hind. Add to that the length of neck and head and you get a creature not much less than two feet long. But now observe this other measurement. The animal has been moving and we have the length of its stride. In each case it is only about three inches. You have an indication, you see, of a long body with very short legs attached to it. It can run up a curtain and it is carnivorous.'

'How do you arrive at that?'

'A canary's cage was hanging in the window. It ran up the curtain and its aim seems to have been to get at the bird. It was probably some creature of the weasel and stoat tribe—and yet it is larger than any of these that I have seen.

'We have learned a good deal. We know that a man stood in the road watching the quarrel between the Barclays—the blinds were up and the room lit. We also know that he ran across the lawn, entered the room, accompanied by a strange animal and that he either struck the colonel or, as is equally possible, that the colonel fell down from sheer fright at the sight of him and cut his head on the corner of the fender. Finally, we know that the intruder carried away the key with him when he left.'

'Your discoveries seem to have left the business more obscure than it was before,' I said.

'Quite so. They undoubtedly showed that the affair was much deeper than was at first guessed.

'It is quite certain that when Mrs Barclay left the house she was on good terms with her husband. The coachman heard her chatting with the colonel in a friendly way. Now, it was equally certain that, immediately on her return, she had gone to the room in which she was least likely to see her husband, had flown to tea as an agitated woman will and finally, on his appearance, had broken into violent charges. Therefore something had occurred between seven-thirty and nine o'clock which had completely changed her feelings towards him. But Miss Morrison had been with her during the whole time. It was absolutely certain, therefore, in spite of her denial, that she must know something of the matter.

'I took the obvious course, therefore, of calling upon Miss M, of explaining to her that I was certain that she held the facts in her control and of assuring persuading her that her friend, Mrs Barclay, might find herself in prison with a death penalty unless the matter was cleared up.

'Miss Morrison does not lack cleverness and common sense. She sat thinking for some time after I had spoken and then, turning to me with a quick air of resolution, she broke into a remarkable statement which I will shorten for your benefit.

"I promised my friend that I would say nothing of the matter" she said, "but if I can really help her when so serious a charge is laid against her then I think I am absolved from my promise. I will tell you exactly what happened on Monday evening.

"We were returning from the Watt Street Mission at about a quarter to nine. On our way we had to pass through Hudson Street, which is a very quiet thoroughfare. I saw a man with a bent back coming towards us, with a box slung over one of his shoulders. He appeared to be deformed. We were passing him when he raised his face to look at us and as he did so he stopped and screamed out in a terrible voice, 'My God, it's Nancy!' Mrs Barclay turned as white as death and would have fallen down had the dreadful-looking creature not caught hold of her. I was going to call for the police, but she, to my surprise, spoke quite civilly to the fellow.

'I thought you had been dead for thirty years, Henry,' she said, in a shaking voice.

'So I have,' he replied. He had a very dark scary face and a shine in his eyes that haunts me in my dreams. There were grey strands in his hair and whiskers and his face was all crinkled like a withered apple.

'Just walk on a little way, dear,' said Mrs Barclay, 'I want to have a word with this man. There is nothing to be afraid of.' She tried to speak boldly, but she was still deadly pale and her lips were trembling.

"I did as she asked me and they talked together for a few minutes. Then she came down the street with her eyes blazing. She never said a word until we were at the door here, when she took me by the hand and begged me to tell no one what had happened.

'It's an old acquaintance of mine who has come down in the world,' she said. When I promised her I would say nothing she kissed me and I have never seen her since. I have now told you the whole truth."

'Watson, her statement was like a light on a dark night. Everything which had been disconnected before began to fall into place. My next step obviously was to find the man whom Mrs Barclay had met. There are not many civilians in Aldershot and a deformed man was sure to have attracted attention. By evening—this very evening, Watson—I found him. The man's name is Henry Wood and he lives in the same street in which the ladies met him. He has been there for only five days. Appearing as a registration agent I chatted with his landlady. The man is by trade a conjurer and performer, entertaining at canteens after nightfall. He carries a creature with him in that box, which the landlady was a little afraid of because she had never seen an animal like it. He uses it in some of his tricks according to her. He seems to speak in a strange tongue sometimes and for the last two nights she had heard him groaning and weeping in his bedroom. As far as money went, he had once given her what looked like a bad coin. She showed it to me, Watson, and it was an Indian rupee.

'So now, my dear fellow, you see exactly how we stand and why it is I want you. It is perfectly plain that after the ladies parted from this man he followed them at a distance. He saw the quarrel between husband and wife through the window, rushed in and the creature which he carried in his box got loose. That is all very certain. But he is the only person in this world who can tell us exactly what happened in that room.'

'And you intend to ask him?'

'Yes—but in the presence of a witness.'

'If he can clear the matter up, it's well and good. If he refuses, we have no alternative but to apply for a warrant. I have one of my Baker Street boys mounting guard over him. We shall find him in Hudson Street tomorrow, Watson. Now, I will be the criminal if I kept you out of bed any longer.'

We arrived at the scene of the tragedy at midday, and, under my companion's guidance, we made our way at once to Hudson Street.

'This is the street,' he said, as we turned into a short thoroughfare lined with plain two-storied brick houses. 'Ah, here is Simpson to report.'

'He's inside, Mr Holmes,' cried a small boy, running up to us.

'Good, Simpson!' said Holmes, patting him on the head. 'Come along, Watson. This is the house.'

He sent in his card with a message that he had come on important business and a moment later we were face to face with the man whom we had come to see. In spite of the warm weather he was bending down over a fire and the little room was like an oven. The man sat all twisted and huddled in his chair in a way which gave an indescribable impression of deformity, but the face which he turned towards us, though worn, must at some time have been quite handsome. He

looked suspiciously at us now out of sickly eyes, and, without speaking or rising, he waved towards two chairs.

'Mr Henry Wood, returned from India, I believe,' said Holmes, friendly. 'I've come over this little matter of Colonel Barclay's death.'

'What should I know about that?'

'That's what I want to find out. You know, I suppose, that unless the matter is cleared up, Mrs Barclay, who is an old friend of yours, will in all probability be tried for murder.'

The man gave a violent start.

'I don't know who you are,' he cried, 'nor how you come to know what you do know, but will you swear that this is true that you tell me?'

'They are only waiting for her to come to her senses to arrest her.'

'My God! Are you in the police yourself?'

'No.'

'What business is it of yours, then?'

'It's every man's business to see justice done. Who killed Colonel James Barclay?'

'It was fate that killed him. But, if I had knocked his brains out, as I wanted to, he would have had no more than his due. His own guilty moral sense struck him down. You want me to tell the story.

'Well, sir, you see me now with my back like a camel and my ribs all twisted, but there was a time when Corporal Henry Wood was the smartest man in the 117th infantry regiment. We were in India then, in cantonments, at a place we'll call Bhurtee. Barclay, who died the other day, was sergeant in the same company as me and Nancy Devoy, the daughter of the colour-sergeant, was the finest girl that ever lived. There were two men that loved her, and one that she loved, and you'll smile when I tell you, was this poor thing huddled before the fire.

'Well, though I had won her heart, her father was set upon her marrying Barclay. I was a

careless lad, while he was educated and ready for promotion. Then the Mutiny broke out and all hell was loose in the country.

'We were shut up in Bhurtee, the regiment, a company of Sikhs along with civilians and womenfolk. There were 10,000 rebels around us. In the second week of the mutiny our water was over and we were wondering whether we could communicate with General Neill's column, which was moving up country. It was our only chance since we could not hope to fight our way out with all the women and children. So I freely offered to go out and to warn General Neill of our danger. My offer was accepted and I talked it over with Sergeant Barclay, who was supposed to know the ground better than any other man and who drew

up a route by which I might get through the rebel lines. At ten o'clock that night I started on my journey.

'My path ran down a dried-up stream, which we hoped would screen me from the enemy's sentries but as I crept around I walked right into six of them, who were bending down in the dark waiting for me. In an instant I was shocked with a blow to my head and tied hand and foot. But the real blow was to my heart because when I regained consciousness I heard enough of their talk to understand that my friend, the very man who had drawn my path, had cheated me by means of a native servant into the hands of the enemy.

'Well, there's no need for me to think about on that part of it. You know now what James Barclay was capable of. Bhurtee was relieved by Neill the

next day but the rebels took me away with them in their retreat and many years passed before I saw a British man again. I was tortured and tried to get away and was captured and tortured again. You can see for yourselves the state in which I was left. Some of them that fled into Nepal took me with them and later I crossed Darjeeling. The hill-folk up there murdered the rebels, who had me, and I became their slave until I escaped. I headed north, until I found myself among the Afghans. There I wandered about for many years and at last came back to Punjab, where I lived mostly among the natives and made a living by performing the conjuring tricks that I had learned. Of what use was it for me, a wretched cripple, to go back to England? Even my desire for revenge could not make me do that. I rather wished that Nancy and my old pals should think of Harry Wood as being dead with a straight back, than see him living and crawling with a stick like a chimpanzee. I heard that Barclay had married Nancy and that he was rising rapidly in the regiment, but even that did not make me speak.

'But when one gets old one has a urged for home. At last I bent on to see the bright green

fields and the hedges of England before I died. I saved enough to bring me across and then I came here where the soldiers are because I know their ways and how to amuse them. So I earn enough to keep me alive.'

'Your narrative is most interesting,' said Holmes. 'I have already heard of your meeting with Mrs Barclay and your mutual acceptance. You then, as I understand, followed her home and saw an argument between her husband and her. Your own feelings overcame you and you ran across the lawn and broke in on them.'

'I did, sir, and at the sight of me he looked as I have never seen a man look before and over he went with his head on the fender. But I read death on his face before he fell. The bare sight of me was like a bullet through his guilty heart.'

'And then?'

'Then Nancy fainted and I took the key of the door from her hand, intending to unlock it and get help. But then it struck me that it was better to leave it alone and run away since things might go against me. In my haste I thrust the key into my pocket and dropped my stick while I was chasing

Teddy, who had run up the curtain. When I got him into his box, from which he had slipped, I was off as fast as I could run.'

'Who's Teddy?' asked Holmes.

The man leaned over and pulled up a cage from the corner. In an instant out slipped a beautiful reddish-brown creature, thin and lithe, a long thin nose and a pair of the finest red eyes that I ever saw in an animal's head.

'It's a mongoose,' I cried.

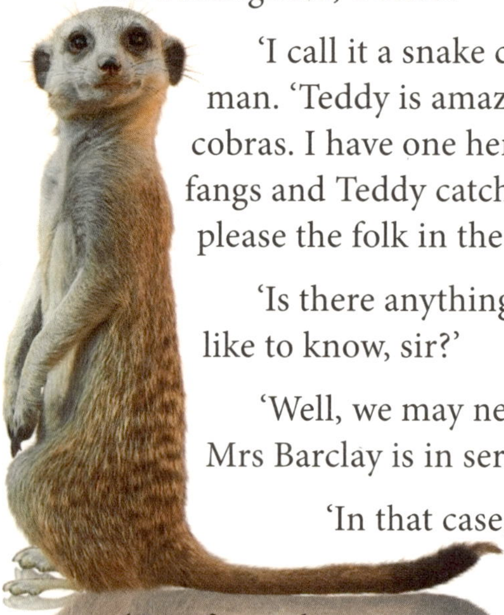

'I call it a snake catcher,' said the man. 'Teddy is amazingly quick on cobras. I have one here without the fangs and Teddy catches it every night to please the folk in the canteen.'

'Is there anything else you would like to know, sir?'

'Well, we may need you again if Mrs Barclay is in serious trouble.'

'In that case, of course, I would come forward.'

'But if not, there is no need to rake up this scandal against a dead man, badly though he has acted. You have at least the satisfaction of knowing that for thirty years of his life his moral sense bitterly scolded him for this wicked action.

Ah, there goes Major Murphy on the other side of the street. Goodbye, Wood. I want to learn if anything has happened since yesterday.'

We were in time to overtake the major before he reached the corner.

'Ah, Holmes,' he said. 'I suppose you have heard that all this fuss has come to nothing?'

'What then?'

'The search is just over. The medical evidence showed conclusively that death was due to a stroke. You see it was quite a simple case after all.'

'Oh, remarkably superficial,' said Holmes, smiling. 'Come, Watson, I don't think we shall be wanted in Aldershot anymore.'

The Adventure of the Greek Interpreter

Arthur Conan Doyle

During my long and close friendship with Mr Sherlock Holmes I had never heard him refer to his relations and hardly ever to his early life. This led me to sometimes regard him as a lonely wonder, a brain without a heart, as lacking in human sympathy as he was superior in intelligence. His complete suppression of every reference to his own people had led me to believe that he was an orphan with no living relatives. One day, to my very great surprise, he began to talk to me about his brother.

It was after tea on a summer evening when our conversation turned to the question of hereditary aptitudes. The point under discussion was how far any particular gift in an individual was due to his ancestry and how far due to his own early training.

'In your own case,' I said, 'from all that you have told me, it seems obvious that your faculty of observation and your peculiar facility for deduction are due to your own systematic training.'

'To some extent,' Holmes answered, thoughtfully. 'However, it is also perhaps in my veins, and may have come with my grandmother, who was the sister of Vernet, the French artist. Art in the blood is liable to take the strangest forms.'

'But how do you know that it is hereditary?'

'Because my brother Mycroft had it in a larger degree than I do.'

This was news to me indeed. If there was another man with such outstanding powers in England, how was it that neither police nor public had heard of him? I suggested that it was my companion's modesty which made him acknowledge his brother as his superior. Holmes laughed at my suggestion.

'My dear Watson,' he said, 'to the logician all things should be seen exactly as they are and to set too low oneself is as much a departure from truth as to magnify one's own powers. I am speaking the exact and literal truth.'

'Is he younger to you?'

'Seven years older than me.'

'How is it that he is unknown?'

'Oh, he is very well-known in his own circle such as the Diogenes Club. The Diogenes Club is the queerest club in London and Mycroft one of the strangest men. He's there every evening from quarter to five to twenty to eight. It's six now, so if you care for a stroll this beautiful evening I shall be happy to introduce you to him.'

Five minutes later we were in the street, walking towards Regent Circus.

'You wonder,' said my companion, 'why it is that Mycroft does not use his powers for detective work. He is incapable of it. He is my superior in observation and conclusion. But he has neither ambition nor energy. Mycroft will not even go out of his way to prove his own solutions and would rather be considered wrong than take the

trouble to prove himself right. Again and again I have taken a problem to him and have received an explanation which has afterwards proved to be the correct one. And yet he was absolutely incapable of working out the practical points which must be dealt with before a case can be laid before a judge or jury.'

'He is not a detective, then?'

'No, not at all. What is to me a means of livelihood is to him a mere hobby. He has an extraordinary faculty for figures and audits the books in some of the government departments. He takes no other exercise and is not seen anywhere else, except in the Diogenes Club.'

'I have never heard of the name.'

'That's quite likely. There are many men in London, you know, who, some from shyness,

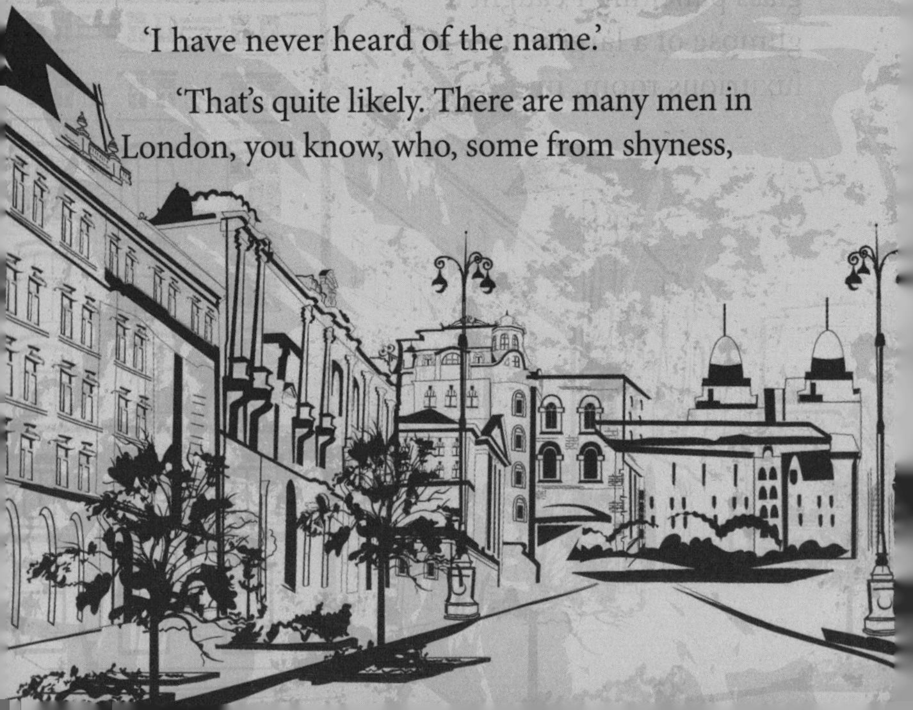

some from misanthropy, have no wish for the company of their fellows. Yet they are not aganist to comfortable chairs and the latest periodicals. It is for the comfort of these that the Diogenes Club was started and it now contains the most unsociable men in town. No member is permitted to take the least notice of another. No talking is, under any circumstances, allowed except in the Stranger's Room. Three offences, if brought to the notice of the committee, render the speaker liable to expulsion.'

We had reached Pall Mall as we talked. Sherlock Holmes stopped at a door, and, cautioning me not to speak, he led the way into the hall. Through the glass panelling I caught a glimpse of a large and luxurious room, in

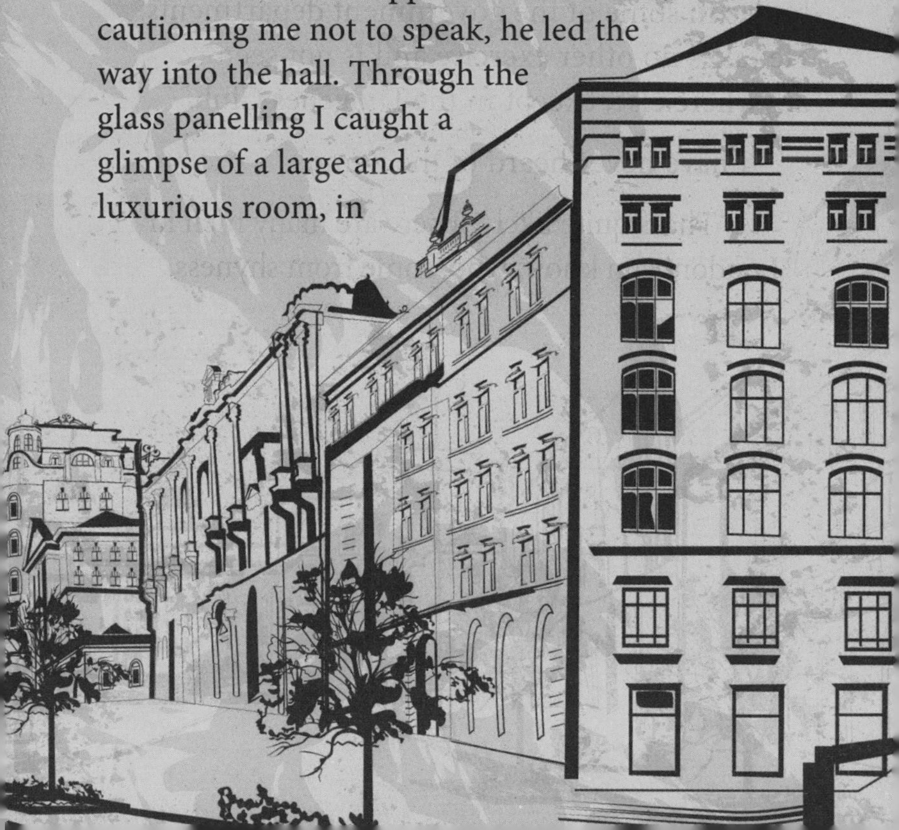

which a considerable number of men were sitting and reading papers, each in his own little nook. Holmes showed me into a small chamber which looked out into Pall Mall, and then, leaving me for a minute, he returned with a companion whom I knew could only be his brother.

Mycroft Holmes was a much larger and heavily build man than Sherlock. His eyes, which were of a strangely light, watery grey, seemed to retain that far away, self-analyzing look which I had only observed in Sherlock's when he was exerting his full powers.

'I am glad to meet you, sir,' he said, putting out a broad fat hand towards me. 'I hear of Sherlock everywhere since you became his chronicler.'

The two sat down together near the window.

'To anyone who wishes to study mankind this is the spot,' said Mycroft. 'Look at the magnificent types! Look at these two men who are coming towards us, for example.'

'The billiard marker and the other?'

'Precisely. What do you make of the other?'

The two men had stopped opposite the window. Some chalk marks over the waistcoat pocket were the only signs of billiards which I could see in one of them. The other was a very small fellow with his hat pushed back and several packages under his arm.

'An old soldier, I realize,' said Sherlock.

'And very recently discharged,' remarked the brother.

'Served in India, I see.'

'And a non-commissioned officer.'

'Royal Artillery, I fancy,' said Sherlock.

'And a widower.'

'But with a child.'

'Children, my dear boy, children.'

'Come,' I said, laughing, 'this is a little too much.'

'Surely,' answered Holmes, 'it is not hard to say that a man with that bearing, expression of authority, and sun-baked skin is a soldier, is more than a private and has not long been away from India.'

'That it hasn't been long since he left the service is clear from the fact that he is still wearing his ammunition boots, as they are called,' observed Mycroft.

'He does not have the cavalry walk, yet it's clear that he wore his hat on one side, as the lighter skin of that side of his eyebrow shows. His weight suggests that he is not a soldier. He is in the artillery.'

'Then, of course, his grief outfit shows that he has lost some one very dear. The fact that he is doing his own shopping looks as though it were his wife. He has been buying things for children. There is a rattle, which shows that one of them is very young. The fact that he has a picture book under his arm shows that there is another child to be thought of.'

I began to understand what my friend meant when he said that his brother had even keener powers that he did himself.

'By the way, Sherlock,' said Mycroft, 'a unique problem has been submitted to me. I really did not have the energy to follow it up. If you would care to hear the facts—'

'My dear Mycroft, I should be delighted.'

Mycroft wrote untidily a note and handed it to the waiter.

'I have asked Mr Melas to step inside,' he said. 'He lodges on the floor above me and I am familiar with him, which led him to come towards me in his confusion. Mr Melas is of Greek descent and is a remarkable linguist. He earns his living partly by acting as a guide to any wealthy visitors who may arrive at the Northumberland Avenue hotels. I will allow him to tell his very remarkable experience in his own way.'

A few minutes later we were joined by a short, stout man with coal-black hair. His dark eyes sparkled with pleasure when he realized that Sherlock Holmes was anxious to hear his story.

'I don't think that the police believe me,' he said in a crying voice. 'Just because they have never heard of it before, they think that such a thing cannot happen. But I know that I shall never be easy in my mind until I know what has become of the poor man with the sticking-plaster on his face.'

'I am all ears,' said Sherlock.

'It was on Monday night—only two days ago—that all this happened,' said Mr Melas. 'I am an interpreter of languages but as I am a Greek by birth, it is with that particular tongue that I am principally related. For many years I have been the chief Greek translator in London and my name is very well-known in the hotels.'

'I'm often called upon at strange hours by foreigners who get into difficulties or by travellers who arrive late and wish my services. I was not surprised, therefore, on Monday night when a Mr Latimer, a very fashionably dressed young man, came up to my apartment and asked me to go along him in a cab which was waiting at the door. A Greek friend had come to see him on business, he said, and as he could speak nothing but his own tongue, the services of an interpreter were necessary. His house was a little distance off, in Kensington, and he hurried me into the cab.'

'We set off once Mr Latimer had seated himself opposite to me. We had come out on Oxford Street and I remarked that this was a roundabout way to Kensington.'

'My companion drew out a most formidable-looking bludgeon from his pocket and switched

it backwards and forward several times, as if to test its weight and strength. Then he placed it without a word on the seat beside him. He drew up the windows on each side and I found to my astonishment that they were covered with paper so as to prevent my seeing through them.'

"I am sorry to cut off your view, Mr Melas," he said. "The fact is that I don't wish you to see where we are going. It might possibly be causing trouble to me if you could find your way there again."

'As you can imagine, I was utterly taken aback. My companion was a powerful broad-shouldered young fellow and I would not have succeeded in a struggle with him.'

"You must be aware that what you are doing is quite illegal, Mr Latimer," I stammered.

"It is a bit of liberty, no doubt," he said in a threatening tone, "but we'll make it up to you. However, I must warn you against trying to raise an alarm, Mr Melas. No one knows where you

are and, whether you are in this carriage or in my house, you are completely in my power."

'I sat in silence and could only wait to see what might happen next. It was a quarter-past seven when we left Pall Mall and according to my watch it was ten minutes to nine when we at last came to a standstill. As I was hurried from the carriage, the door swung open and I found myself inside the house, with a vague idea of a lawn and trees on each side of me as I entered.

'There was a gas lamp inside which was turned so low that I could hardly see anything. In the dim light I could make out that the person who had opened the door was a small, mean-looking, middle-aged man with rounded shoulders. As he turned towards us the glint of the light showed me that he was wearing glasses.

"Is this Mr Melas, Harold?" he asked.

"Yes."

"Well done! No ill-will, Mr Melas, I hope, but we could not get on without you. If you deal fairly with us you'll not regret it, but if you try any tricks, God help you!"

'He spoke in a nervous shaky fashion and with little giggling laughs in between but somehow he influenced me with fear more than the other.

"What do you want with me?" I asked.

"Only to ask a few questions of a Greek gentleman who is visiting us and to let us know the answers. But say no more than you are told to say, or—" here came the nervous giggle again— "you will wish you had never been born."

'As he spoke he opened a door and showed the way into a room which appeared to be very richly furnished, but again it was dimly lit. I caught glimpses of velvet chairs, a high white marble mantelpiece and what seemed to be a suit of Japanese armour on one side.

'The elderly man motioned that I should sit down in a chair. The younger one had left us, but he suddenly returned through another door, leading with him a gentleman clad in a loose dressing gown who moved slowly towards us. As he came into the circle of dim light I was shocked to see him. He was deadly pale and terribly thin, with the sticking-out, brilliant eyes of a man whose spirit was greater than his strength. His face was horribly criss-crossed with sticking plaster, and one large pad of it was attached over his mouth.

"Do you have the slate, Harold?" cried the older man, as this strange being fell rather than sat down in a chair. "Then, give him the pencil. You will ask the questions, Mr Melas, and he will write the answers. First, ask him whether he is prepared to sign the papers?"

'The man's eyes flashed.

"Never!" he wrote in Greek on the slate.

'"On no condition?" I asked, at the bidding of our tyrant.

"Only if I see her married in my presence by a Greek priest whom I know."

'The man giggled in his venomous way.

"Do you know what awaits you, then?"

"I don't care about myself."

'These are samples of the questions and answers which made up our strange half-spoken, half-written conversation. I had to repeatedly ask him whether he would sign the documents. But soon an idea occurred to me. I began adding little sentences of my own to each question, innocent ones at first, to test whether either of our companions could understand, and then, as I found that they showed no signs I played a more dangerous game. Our conversation ran something like this:

"You can achieve no good by this stubbornness. Who are you?"

"I don't care. I am a stranger in London."

"You will be responsible for the result. How long have you been here?"

"Let it be so. Three weeks."

"The property can never be yours. What ails you?"

"It shall not go to villains. They are starving me."

"You shall go free if you sign. What house is this?"

"I will never sign. I do not know."

"You are not doing her any service. What is your name?"

"Let me hear her say so. Kratides."

"You shall see her if you sign. Where are you from?"

"Then I shall never see her. Athens."

'Another five minutes, Mr Holmes, and I would have wormed out the whole story. But at that instant the door opened and a woman stepped into the room. I could only make out that she was tall and graceful, with black hair and clad in a loose white gown.

"Harold," she said, speaking English with a broken accent. "I could not stay away longer. It is so lonely up there with only—Oh, my God, it is Paul!"

'The man with a convulsive effort tore the plaster from his lips, and screaming out "Sophy! Sophy!" rushed into the woman's arms. Their hug was but for an instant, however, for the younger man seized the woman and pushed her out of the room, while the elder easily overpowered his thin victim and dragged him away through the other door.

"That will do, Mr Melas," said the older man, returning quickly. "You can see that we have taken you into our confidence over some very private business. We would not have troubled you, but our friend who speaks Greek and who began these discussions has been forced to return to the East."

"Here are five sovereigns," he said, walking up to me, "which will, I hope, be a sufficient fee. But remember," he added, tapping me lightly on the chest and giggling, "if you speak to anyone about this then, may God have mercy on you!"

'I cannot tell you the loathing and horror with which this insignificant-looking man inspired me. His steel grey eyes shined with a deadly rigid cruelty in their depths.

"Now you will find the carriage waiting and my friend will help you return."

'I was hurried through the hall and into the vehicle. We rode in silence with the windows raised, until just after midnight, the carriage stopped.

"You will get down here, Mr Melas," said my companion. "I am sorry to leave you so far from your house, but there is no alternative."

'He opened the door as he spoke and as soon as I stepped out the carriage rattled away. Far away I could see a line of houses, with a light here and there in the upper windows. I stood looking around when I saw someone coming towards me in the darkness. I realized that he was a railway porter.

"Can you tell me what place this is?" I asked.

"Wandsworth Common," he said.

"Can I get a train to town?"

"If you walk on a mile or so to Clapham Junction," he said, "you'll be in time for the last to Victoria."

'So that was the end of my adventure, Mr Holmes. I want to help that unhappy man if I can. I have informed the police as well.'

We all sat in silence for some time after listening to this amazing story. Then Sherlock looked across at his brother.

'Any steps?' he asked.

Mycroft picked up the *Daily News*, which was lying on the side table.

'An advertisement had been placed in all the dailies stating that anybody who provides any information to the whereabouts of a Greek gentleman named Paul Kratides, from Athens, or a Greek lady named Sophy, will be rewarded. No answer.'

'How about sending a telegram to the head of the Athens police?'

'Sherlock has all the energy of the family,' said Mycroft, turning to me. 'Well, you take the case up by all means and let me know if you do any good.'

'Certainly,' answered my friend, rising from his chair. 'I'll let you and Mr Melas know.'

Sherlock advised Mr Melas to be on his guard and then we left. As we walked home together, Holmes stopped at a telegraph office and sent off several telegrams.

'You see, Watson,' he remarked, 'our evening has by no means been wasted. There can be only one explanation for the problem which we have just heard although there are still some lose ends. You must have formed some theory which will explain the facts as well.'

'Yes, in a vague way. It seemed obvious to me that this Greek girl had been carried off by the young Englishman named Harold Latimer.'

'Carried off from where?'

'Athens, perhaps.'

Sherlock Holmes shook his head.

'This young man could not speak a word of Greek. The lady could speak English fairly well. Inference—she had been in England for some time but he had not been to Greece.'

'Well, then, we will think that she had come on a visit to England and that this Harold had persuaded her to fly with him.'

'That is more probable.'

'Then the brother—that, I imagine, must be the relationship—comes over from Greece to interfere. He carelessly puts himself into the power of the young man and his older associate. They use violence towards him in order to make him sign some papers to seize the girl's fortune—

of which he may be trustee. This he refuses to do. In order to work out with him they have to get an interpreter and they hire Mr Melas, having used someone else before. The girl is not told about her brother's arrival and finds out by accident.'

'Excellent, Watson!' cried Holmes. 'I think that you are not far from the truth. If they give us time we can arrest them.'

'But how can we find where this house lies?'

'Well, if our guess is correct and the girl's name is or was Sophy Kratides, we shall be able to trace her. That must be our main hope because the brother is a complete stranger. It is clear that some time has passed by since this Harold established these relations with the girl—some weeks, at any rate—since the brother in Greece has had time to hear of it and come across. If they have been living in the same place during this time, it is probable that we shall have some answer to Mycroft's advertisement.'

We had reached our house in Baker Street while we had been talking. When we entered our room to our great surprise we found Mycroft sitting in the armchair.

'Come in!' he said mildly, smiling at our surprised faces. 'You don't expect such energy from me, do you, Sherlock? But somehow this case attracts me.'

'How did you get here?'

'I passed you in a carriage. I received an answer to my advertisement, a few minutes after you left.'

Mycroft Holmes took out a sheet of paper.

'Here it is,' he said, 'written on royal cream paper by a middle-aged man with a weak constitution.

Sir,

In answer to your advertisement today, I beg to inform you that I know the young lady in question very well. If you should care to call on me I could give you some particulars as to her painful history. She is living at present at The Myrtles, Beckenham.

Yours faithfully,

J Davenport.

'He writes from Lower Brixton,' said Mycroft. 'Shall we drive to him now, Sherlock?'

'My dear Mycroft, the brother's life is more valuable than the sister's story. I think we should call at Scotland Yard for Inspector Gregson and go straight out to Beckenham.'

'Better pick up Mr Melas on our way,' I suggested. 'We may need an interpreter.'

'Excellent,' said Sherlock. 'Send the boy for a four-wheeler and we shall be off at once.' He opened a drawer as he spoke and I noticed that he slipped his revolver into his pocket.

'Yes,' he said, in answer to my glance. 'I should say from what we have heard, that we are dealing with a particularly dangerous gang.'

It was almost dark before we found ourselves outside Mr Melas's rooms. A gentleman had just called for him and he had left.

'Can you tell me where?' asked Mycroft.

'I don't know, sir,' answered the woman who had opened the door, 'I only know that he drove away with the gentleman in a carriage.'

'Did the gentleman give a name?'

'No, sir.'

'Was he a tall, handsome, dark young man?'

'Oh, no, sir. He was a little gentleman, with glasses and a thin face. He was laughing all the time that he was talking.'

'Come along!' cried Sherlock Holmes, abruptly. 'This grows serious,' he observed, as we drove to Scotland Yard. 'These men have got hold of Melas again. No doubt they want his professional services, but, having used him, they may be willing to punish him for what they will regard as his treachery.'

We hoped that, by taking train, we might reach Beckenham sooner than the carriage. On reaching Scotland Yard, however, it was more than an hour before we could get Inspector Gregson and comply with the legal formalities which would enable us to enter the house. It was half-past ten before the four of us stepped out on the Beckenham platform. We took a cab to The Myrtles—a large dark house standing away from the road.

'Our birds have flown and the nest is empty,' said Holmes when we reached there.

'Why do you say so?' asked the inspector.

'A carriage heavily loaded with luggage has passed out during the last hour. You may have observed the wheel tracks going up to the house. But the

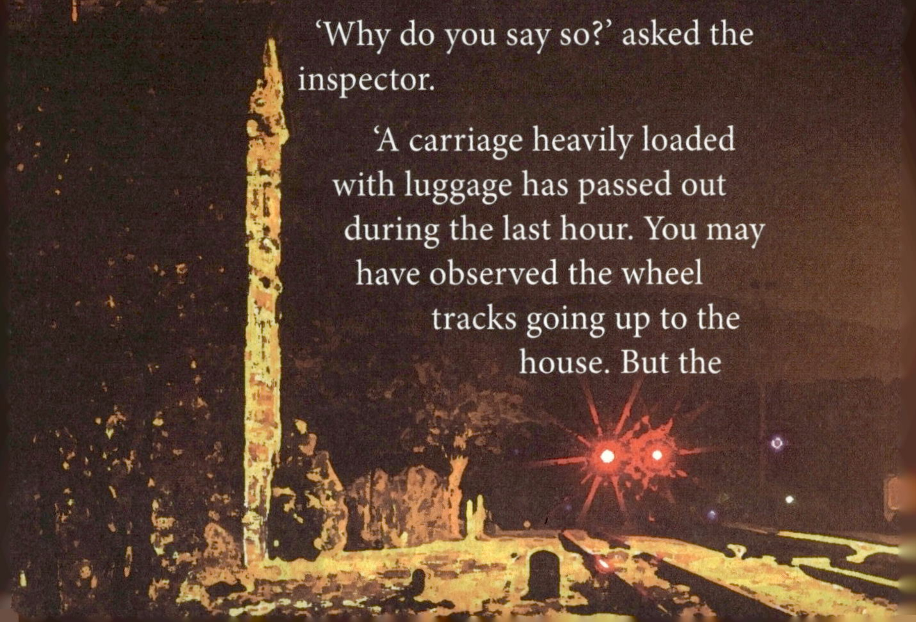

outward bound ones were very much deeper so that we can say with certainty that there was a very large weight on the carriage.'

'It will not be an easy door to force open, but we will try if we cannot get someone to hear us,' said the inspector.

He hammered loudly at the knocker and rang the bell, but without any success. Holmes had slipped away but he came back in a few minutes.

'I have opened up a window,' he said.

'Well, I think that under the circumstances we may enter without an invitation,' remarked the inspector.

One after the other we made our way into a large apartment, which was evidently that in which Mr Melas had found himself. The inspector had lit his lantern and by its light we could see the

two doors, the curtain, the lamp and the suit of Japanese armour as he had described them.

'What is that?' asked Holmes, suddenly.

We all stood still and listened. A low moaning sound was coming from upstairs. Holmes rushed up and we followed. There were three doors on the second floor and it was from the central one that the evil sounds could be heard, sinking sometimes into a dull murmur and rising again into a high cry. It was locked, but the key had been left on the outside. Holmes flung open the door and rushed in but he was out again in an instant, with his hand to his throat.

'It's charcoal,' he cried. 'Give it time. It will clear.'

Looking in, we could see that the only light in the room came from a dull blue flame from a small brass tripod in the centre. In the shadows

beyond we saw the vague loom of two figures which bend against the wall. From the open door there smell strongly of a horrible poisonous exhalation which set us fighting for breath and coughing. Dashing into the room again, Holmes threw up the window and hurled the tripod out into the garden.

'We can enter in a minute,' he fought for breath, darting out again. 'Hold the light at the door and we shall get them out, Mycroft, now!'

With a rush we got to the poisoned men and dragged them out into the hall. Both of them were unconscious, with swollen faces and blue lips. One of them was our Greek interpreter and the other was a tall man in the last stage of thinness, with sticking plaster over his face. A glance showed me that for him at least our aid had come too late. Mr Melas, however, still lived and in less than an hour opened his eyes.

The story which he told us confirmed our own conclusions. Mr Melas's visitor, after threatening him with death, had kidnapped him for the second time. He had been brought to Beckenham and had acted as interpreter in a second interview, in which the two Englishmen had threatened their prisoner with instant death if he did not comply with their demands. Finally, they had thrown him back into his prison and after scolding Melas with his treachery, which appeared from the newspaper advertisement, they had stunned him with a blow from a stick. He had remained unconscious until he found us bending over him.

And this was the case of the Grecian Interpreter, the explanation of which is still involved in some mystery. By communicating with the gentleman who had answered the advertisement, we learnt that the unfortunate young lady was of a wealthy Greek family and that she was visiting some friends in England. While there she had met a young man named Harold Latimer, who had persuaded her to fly with him. Her friends, shocked at the event, had contented themselves with informing her brother at Athens, and had then washed their hands of the matter. The brother, on his arrival in England, had imprudently placed himself in the power of Latimer and of his associate, whose name was Wilson Kemp. They kept him a prisoner and tried to make him sign away his own and his sister's property. They had kept him in the house without the girl's knowledge and the plaster over the face had been to make recognition difficult in case she should ever catch a glimpse of him. She, however, had instantly seen through the disguise when, on the occasion of the interpreter's visit, she had seen him for the first time. Realizing that their secret was out, and that their prisoner was not to be pressurized, the two villains had fled with the girl at a few hours' notice from the furnished house which they had hired, having first, taken vengeance on both the captive men.

Many months later a curious newspaper cutting reached us from Budapest. It told how two Englishmen who had been travelling with a woman had met with a tragic end. They had each been stabbed, it seems, and the Hungarian police were of opinion that they had quarrelled and had caused mortal injuries upon each other. Holmes, however, was, I fancy, of a different opinion. He believed that, if one could find the Greek girl, one might learn how the wrongs against her and her brother were avenged.

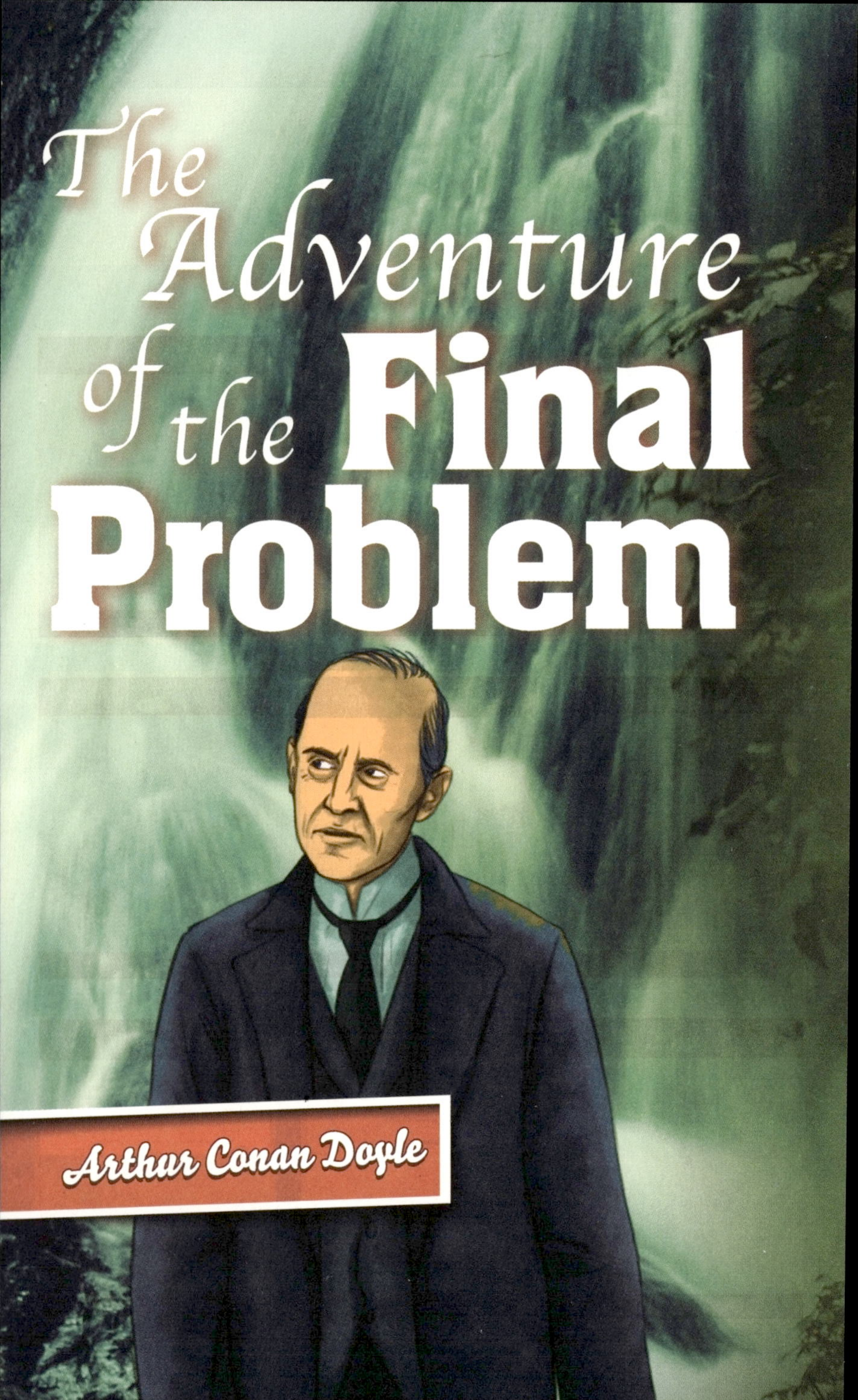
The Adventure of the Final Problem
Arthur Conan Doyle

It is with a heavy heart that I take up my pen to record my friend Mr Sherlock Holmes' extraordinary gifts for the last time. Previously, I have tried to give some account of my strange experiences in his company, beginning with the 'Study in Scarlet' up to the time of his involvement in the matter of the 'Naval Treaty.' It was my intention to stop there and to have said nothing of that event which has created a void in my life which the lapse of two years has done little to fill. However, the recent letters in which Colonel James Moriarty defends the memory of his brother force me to lay the facts before the public exactly as they occurred. I alone know the absolute truth of the matter and no good purpose is served by its suppression. As far as I know, there have been only three accounts in the public press: that in the Journal de Genève on 6 May 1891, the Reuter's despatch in the English papers on 7 May and finally the recent letter to which I have referred to. Of these the first and second were extremely concise, while the last is an absolute distortion of the facts. It is, therefore, up to me to tell for the first time what really took place between Professor Moriarty and Mr Sherlock Holmes.

After my marriage and my subsequent start in private practice, my relation with Holmes was to some extent changed. He still came to me from time to time when he desired a companion in his investigation but these occasions grew more and more seldom. In the winter of 1890 and the early spring of 1891, I saw in the papers that he had been engaged by the French government upon a matter of supreme importance and I received two notes from Holmes from which I gathered that his stay in France was likely to be a long one. It was with some surprise, therefore, that I saw him walk into my consulting room on the evening of 24 April. He was looking even paler and thinner than usual.

'Do you mind my closing the shutters?' he asked as he edged his way around and bolted the shutters tightly.

'Are you afraid of something?' I asked.

'Well, I am.'

'Of what?'

'Of airguns.'

'My dear Holmes, what do you mean?'

'I think that you know me well enough, Watson, to understand that I am by no means a nervous man. At the same time, it is stupidity rather than courage to refuse to recognize danger when it is close upon you. I must apologize for calling so late,' he continued, 'and I hope you'll allow me, later, to leave your house by climbing over your back garden wall.'

'But what does it all mean?' I asked.

'Is Mrs Watson in?'

'She is away.'

'Oh! Then it makes it easier for me to propose that you should come away with me for a week.'

'Where?'

'Oh, anywhere. It's all the same to me.'

There was something very strange in all this. It was not Holmes's nature to take an aimless holiday and something about his pale worn face told me that his nerves were at their highest tension. He saw the question in my eyes, and, putting his fingertips together, he explained the situation.

'You have probably never heard of Professor Moriarty?' he said.

'Never.'

'Yes, that's a stroke of genius!' he cried. 'The man pervades London and no one has heard of him. That's what puts him on a top in the crime records. I tell you, Watson, in all seriousness, that if I could free society of that man, I should feel

that my own career had reached its summit and I shall be prepared to retire. But I could not rest, Watson, if I knew that such a man as Professor Moriarty is walking the streets of London unchallenged.'

'What has he done, then?'

'His career has been an extraordinary one. He was born into a good family, has received excellent education and is gifted with a amazing mathematical faculty. He won the Mathematical Chair at one of our smaller universities and had a most brilliant career before him. But a criminal strain runs in his blood, which was rendered infinitely more dangerous by his extraordinary mental powers. Dark rumours about him eventually compelled him to resign his chair and to come down to London, where he set up as an army coach. So much is known to the world

but what I am telling you now is what I have discovered myself.

'For many years I have been conscious of a deep organizing power which stands in the way of the law, and throws its shield over the wrongdoer. Again and again in cases of the most varying sorts—forgery cases, robberies, murders—I have felt the presence of this force. At last the time came when I seized my thread and followed it, until it led me to ex-Professor Moriarty.

'He is the organizer of half that is evil and of nearly all that is undetected in this great city. He has a brain of the first order. He only plans. But his agents are numerous and splendidly organized. Is there a crime to be done, a paper to be abstracted, a man to be removed—the word is passed to the Professor, the matter is organized and carried out. The agent may be caught. In that case money is found for his bail or his defence. But the central power which uses the agent is never caught—never so much as suspected. This was the organization which I deduced, Watson, and which I devoted my whole energy to exposing and breaking up.

'But it seemed impossible to get evidence. After three months I was forced to admit that I had at last met an enemy who was my intellectual equal. But then he slipped when I was so close upon him. I have now woven my net around him until it is all ready to close. In three days—that is to say, next Monday—matters will be ripe, and the Professor, with all the principal members of his gang, will be in the hands of the police. However, if we move at all too soon they may slip out of our hands.

'Now, if I could have done this without the knowledge of Professor Moriarty, all would have been well. But he is too shrewd for that. He saw every step which I took to draw my toils round him. This morning, I was sitting in my room thinking the matter over, when the door opened and Professor Moriarty stood before me.

'Watson, I must admit that I was shocked to see the man whom I had been thinking about standing there at my door. He is extremely tall and thin, his forehead domes out in a white curve, and his eyes are deeply sunken in his head. He is clean-shaven, pale and retains something of the professor in his features. His shoulders are rounded and his face sticks out forward. He peered at me with great curiosity in his puckered eyes.

"You have less frontal development than I expected," he said, at last. "It is a dangerous habit to finger loaded firearms in the pocket of one's dressing gown."

'The fact is that when he entered I recognized the extreme danger in which I lay. The only way he could escape was by silencing me. In an instant I had slipped the revolver from the drawer into my pocket. At his remark I drew the weapon out and placed it on the table.

"You evidently don't know me," he said with a smile.

"On the contrary," I answered, "I think it is fairly evident that I do. Please take a chair. I can spare you five minutes if you have anything to say."

"All that I have to say has already crossed your mind," he said.

"Then my answer must have crossed yours," I replied.

"You stand fast?"

"Absolutely."

'He clapped his hand into his pocket and I raised the pistol from the table. But he merely drew out a notebook in which he had written untidily some dates.

"You crossed my path on the 4th of January,' he said. "By the middle of February I was seriously troubled by you; at the end of March I was absolutely delayed in my plans; and now, at the close of April, I find that because of your continual persecution I am in danger of losing my liberty. The situation is becoming an impossible one."

"Do you have any suggestions?" I asked.

"You must drop it, Mr Holmes," he said.

"I am quite sure that a man of your intelligence will see that there can be only one outcome to this affair," he said. "It is necessary that you should

withdraw. It has been an intellectual treat to me to see the way in which you have grappled with this affair and it would grieve me to be forced to take any extreme measure."

"Danger is a part of my trade," I remarked.

"It shall be unavoidable destruction," he said. "You stand in the way not merely of an individual, but of a mighty organization."

"I am afraid," I said, rising, "that in the pleasure of this conversation I am neglecting business of importance which awaits me elsewhere."

"Well, well," he said, rising at last. "It's a pity, but I have done what I could. I know every move of your game. You can do nothing before Monday. If you are clever enough to bring destruction upon me, rest assured that I shall do as much to you."

"If I am assured of the former eventuality I would, in public interest, cheerfully accept the latter."

"I can promise you one, but not the other," he spoke roughly and left the room.

'That was my interview with Professor Moriarty. His speech leaves a declaration of sincerity which a mere bully could not produce. Of course, you will say, "Why not take police

precautions against him?" the reason is that I am well convinced that it is from his agents that the blow will fall. I went out at about midday on some business in Oxford Street. As I passed the corner which leads to the Welbeck Street crossing, a furiously driven two-horse van moved quickly around and was on to me like a flash. I jumped on the footpath and saved myself by a fraction of a second. The van disappeared in an instant. I kept to the pavement after that, Watson, but as I walked down Vere Street a brick dropped down from the roof of one of the houses and shattered at my feet. I called the police and had the place examined. There were bricks piled up on the roof for some repairs and they wanted me to believe that the wind had toppled over one of these. I could not prove anything. I took a carriage

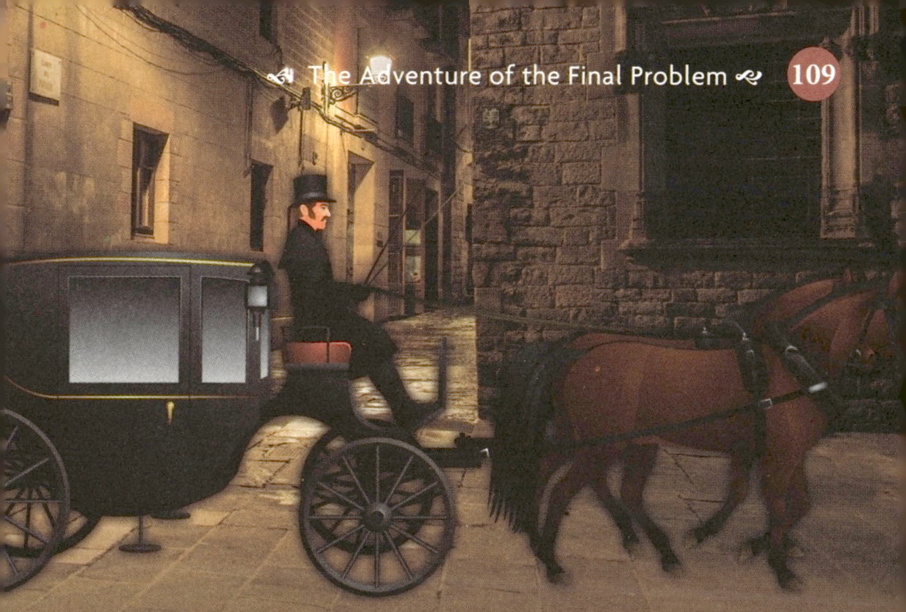

after that and reached my brother's room in Pall Mall, where I spent the day. Now I have come to you, and on my way I was attacked by a man with a bludgeon. I knocked him down and the police have him in custody but I can tell you that no connection will ever be made between the attacker and Professor Moriarty.'

I admired my friend's courage as he sat quietly checking off a series of incidents which must have made up a day of horror.

'Will you will spend the night here?' I asked.

'No, my friend, you might find me a dangerous guest. I have laid my plans and all will be well. As far as the arrest goes, matters can move without my help. My presence is only necessary for a declaration. Therefore, I need to get away for a few days before the police are at liberty to act. It would be a great pleasure to me, therefore, if you could come with me.'

'I should be glad to come,' I said.

'Then we shall start tomorrow morning. Now listen! We are up against the cleverest villian and the most powerful group of criminals in Europe. You will send off your unaddressed luggage, by a trusty messenger to Victoria tonight. In the morning you will send for a carriage, in which you will ride to the Strand end of the Lowther Arcade, handing the address to the cabman on a slip of paper, with a request that he will not throw it away. Dash through the Arcade and reach the other side at a quarter-past nine. You will find another carriage waiting, driven by a fellow with a heavy black cloak tipped at the collar with red. Step into this, and you will reach Victoria in time for the *Continental Express*.'

'Where shall I meet you?'

'At the station. The second first-class carriage from the front will be reserved for us.'

After this set of instructions, Holmes left, as planned, by climbing over the back wall.

In the morning I reached Victoria Station as directed. My luggage was waiting for me and I had no difficulty in finding the carriage which

Holmes had indicated. However, I could see no sign of Holmes yet. The station clock showed that the train was due to leave in only seven minutes. I spent a few minutes in assisting an Italian priest, who was trying to make a porter understand, in his broken English, that his luggage had to be checked through to Paris. On returning to my carriage I found that the porter, in spite of the ticket, had seated the Italian priest there. I shrugged my shoulders quietly and continued to look out anxiously for my friend. I was afraid that his absence might mean that some blow had fallen upon him during the night. The doors were shut and the whistle blown, when—

'My dear Watson,' said a voice, 'you have not even wished me good morning.'

I turned in out of control astonishment. The aged ecclesiastic had turned his face towards me. The wrinkles smoothed, the nose drew away from the chin, the lower lip stopped to stick out and the mouth to murmer, the dull eyes regained their fire and the hanging figure expanded.

'Good heavens!' I cried. 'You startled me!'

'Every precaution is still necessary,' he whispered. 'I have reason to believe that they are hot on our trail. Ah, there is Moriarty himself.'

The train had already begun to move as Holmes spoke. Glancing back, I saw a tall man pushing his way furiously through the crowd. However, it was too late for we were rapidly gathering momentum and an instant later had shot clear of the station.

'With all our precautions, you see that we have cut it rather fine,' said Holmes, laughing.

'Have you seen the morning paper, Watson?'

'No.'

'They set fire to our rooms last night. No great harm was done.'

'Good heavens, Holmes! This is intolerable.'

'They must have lost my track completely after their bludgeon-man was arrested. They have obviously been watching you, however, and that is what has brought Moriarty to Victoria. We must plan what we are to do about Moriarty now.'

'Since this is an express and a boat runs in connection with it, I think we would have shaken him off our trail.'

'My dear Watson, this train stops at Canterbury and there is always at least a quarter of an hour's delay there. Moriarty will get on a special train and catch us there.'

'One would think that we were the criminals,' I remarked. 'Let us have him arrested on his arrival.'

'That would ruin three months' work. We will catch the big fish but the smaller will rush right and left out of the net. On Monday we should have them all.'

'What shall we do then?'

'We shall get out at Canterbury. Then we must make a cross-country journey to Newhaven, and over to Dieppe. Moriarty will do what I would do. He will get to Paris, locate our luggage and wait for two days at the depot. In the meantime we shall treat ourselves to a couple of carpet bags, purchase necessities along the way and make our way at our leisure into Switzerland, via Luxembourg and Basle.'

So, we got down at Cantebury, only to find that we would have to wait an hour before we could get a train to Newhaven.

I was looking at the rapidly disappearing luggage-van which contained my wardrobe, when Holmes pulled my sleeve and pointed up the line.

'Already, you see,' he said.

Far away, from among the Kentish woods a thin spray of smoke arose. A minute later a carriage and engine were seen coming towards the station. We had hardly time to hide behind a pile of luggage when it passed with a rattle and a roar, beating a blast of hot air into our faces.

'There he goes,' said Holmes, as we watched the carriage. 'There are limits, you see, to our friend's intelligence. It would have been a master stroke had he arrived at what I would deduce and acted accordingly.'

'And what would he have done had he overtaken us?'

'There cannot be the least doubt that he would have attempted a murderous attack on me.'

We made our way to Brussels that night and spent two days there and then moved as far as Strasburg on the third day. On Monday morning Holmes had telegraphed to the London police and in the evening we found a reply waiting for us at our hotel. Holmes tore it open and then with a bitter curse threw it into the fireplace.

'He has escaped!' Holmes groaned.

'Moriarty?'

'They have secured the whole gang with the exception of him. He has given them the slip. Of course, when I had left the country there was no one to cope with him. I think that you had better return to England, Watson.'

'Why?'

'I am a dangerous companion to be around now. This man's occupation is gone. He will devote all his energies to taking revenge against me.'

We argued over this for half an hour, but that night we resumed our journey and were well on our way to Geneva.

Whether in the homely Alpine villages or in the lonely mountain passes, Holmes was convinced that we could not walk ourselves clear of the danger which was haunting our footsteps. Once, I remember, as we walked along the border of the sad Daubensee, a large rock which had been dislodged from the ridge on our right clattered down and roared into the lake behind us. In an instant Holmes had raced up on to the ridge, and, standing upon a lofty pinnacle, craned his neck in every direction. Our guide assured him that it was common for stones to fall during this time at that spot. Holmes said nothing, but he smiled at me suggesting that it is just as he had expected.

And yet for all his watchfulness he was never depressed. On the contrary, I can never recollect having seen him in such exuberant spirits. He repeatedly stated that if he could be assured that society was freed from Professor Moriarty he would cheerfully bring his own career to a conclusion.

'Your memoirs will draw to an end, Watson,' he remarked, 'on the day that I crown my career with the capture or extinction of the most dangerous and capable criminal in Europe.'

I shall be brief, and yet exact, in the little which remains for me to tell. It is not a subject on which I would like to dwell, and yet I am conscious that duty requires that I do not omit any detail.

It was on 3 May that we reached the little village of Meiringen, where we put up at the Englischer Hof. Our landlord was an intelligent man and spoke excellent English. At his advice, on the afternoon of the 4th we set off together, with the intention of crossing the hills and spending the night at the hamlet of Rosenlaui. We were told that we must make a small detour to see the Reichenbach Falls, which are about halfway up the hill.

It is indeed, a scary place. The torrent—swollen by the melting snow—plunges into a huge abyss, from which the spray rolls up like the smoke from a burning house. The shaft into which the river hurls itself is an immense chasm, lined by shining coal-black rock and narrowing into a pit of incalculable depth. We stood near the edge looking down at the gleam of the water far below us and listening to the half-human shout which came booming up with the spray out of the abyss.

The path which provides a view of the fall ends abruptly. We had just turned to make our way back, when we saw a Swiss lad come running along it with a letter in his hand. It bore the mark of the hotel which we had just left and was addressed to me by the landlord. It appeared that within a few minutes of our leaving, an English lady had arrived who was severely ill. She was heading towards Lucerne, when a sudden haemorrhage had overtaken her. It looked like she

could hardly survive a few hours but it would be a great comfort to her to see an English doctor, and, if I would return, etc. The good landlord assured me that he would look upon my compliance as a very great favour, since the lady absolutely refused to see a Swiss physician, and he felt a great responsibility towards her.

It was impossible to refuse the request of a fellow-countrywoman dying in a strange land. Yet I did not wish to leave Holmes. It was finally agreed, however, that the young Swiss messenger would stay with him as guide and companion while I returned to Meiringen. My friend would stay for some time at the fall, he said, and would then walk over the hill to Rosenlaui, where I would join him in the evening. As I turned away I saw Holmes, with his back against a rock and his arms folded, gazing down at the rush of the waters. It was the last that I was ever destined to see of him in this world.

When I was near the bottom of the descent I looked back. It was impossible, from that position, to see the fall, but I could see the curving path which winds over the shoulder of the hill and leads to it. Along this a man was, I remember, walking very rapidly.

I could see his black figure clearly outlined against the green behind him. However, I did

not pay him much attention as I hurried on my errand.

It may have been a little over an hour before I reached Meiringen. The landlord was standing at the porch of his hotel.

'Well,' said I, as I came hurrying up, 'how is she?'

A look of surprise passed over his face, and at the first quiver of his eyebrows my heart turned to lead in my breast.

'You did not write this?' I said, pulling the letter from my pocket. 'There is no sick Englishwoman in the hotel?'

'Certainly not!' he cried. 'But it has the hotel mark upon it! Ha, it must have been written by that tall Englishman who came in after you had gone. He said—'

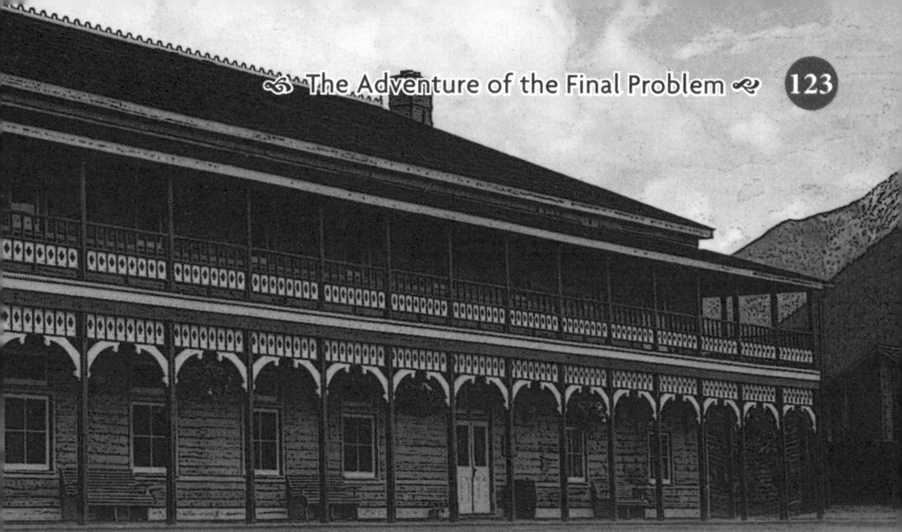

I did not wait for the landlord's explanations but ran down the village street. It had taken me an hour to come down. For all my efforts two more had passed before I found myself at the fall of Reichenbach once more. There was Holmes's Alpine walking stick still leaning against the rock by which I had left him. But there was no sign of him and it was in vain that I shouted. My only answer was my own voice booming in a rolling echo from the cliffs around me.

It was the sight of that Alpine stick which turned me cold and sick. He had not gone to Rosenlaui, then. He had remained on that footpath, with a wall on one side and sheer drop on the other, until his enemy had overtaken him. The young Swiss had gone too. He had probably been in the pay of Moriarty and had left the two men together. And then what had happened? Who was to tell us what had happened then?

I stood for a minute or two to collect myself, for I was dazed with the horror. Then I began to think of Holmes's own methods and to try to practise them in reading this tragedy. It was, alas, only too easy to do. During our conversation we had not gone to the end of the path and the Alpine stick marked the place where we had stood. The blackish soil is kept forever soft by the continuous drift of spray and even a bird would leave its mark on it. Two lines of footprints were clearly marked along the farther end of the path, both leading away from me. There were none returning. A few yards from the end the soil was all ploughed up into a patch of mud and the branches and ferns which grew there were torn and in a mess. I lay upon my face and peered over with the spray spouting up all around me. I could only see here and there the glistening of moisture on the black walls, and far away down at the end of the shaft the gleam of the broken water. I shouted but heard only the same half-human cry of the fall.

It was destined, however, that I should after all have a last word of greeting from my friend and comrade. I have said that his Alpine stick had been left leaning against a rock which jutted on to the path. From the top of this rock the gleam of something bright caught my eye and raising my hand, I found that it came from the silver cigarette case which Holmes used to carry. As I took it up a small piece of paper on which it had been placed fluttered down on to the ground. Unfolding it, I found that it consisted of three pages torn from his notebook and addressed to me. It was characteristic of the man that the writing was firm and clear, as though it had been written in his study.

My dear Watson

I write these few lines through the courtesy of Mr Moriarty, who awaits me for the final discussion of those questions which lie between us. He has been giving me a sketch of the methods by which he avoided the English police and kept himself informed of our movements. They certainly confirm the very high opinion which I had formed of his abilities. I am pleased to think that I shall be able to free society from any further effects of his presence, though I fear that it is at a cost which will give pain to my friends, and especially, my dear Watson, to you. I have already explained to you, however, that my career had in any case reached its crisis and that no possible conclusion to it could be more congenial to me than this. Indeed, I was quite convinced that the letter from Meiringen was a hoax and I allowed you to depart on that errand knowing that some development of this sort would follow. Tell Inspector Patterson that the papers which he needs to convict the gang are in my desk, done up in a blue envelope and inscribed 'Moriarty.' I made every disposition of my property before leaving England and handed it to my brother Mycroft. Please give my greetings to Mrs Watson and believe me to be, my dear fellow,

Very sincerely yours,

Sherlock Holmes